# DRAGON SIGN

2ND EDITION

by

Kevin D. Finson

**Dedicated to Savannah for her love and vivid imagination of life and of what is possible.**

© by Finson, 2024. All rights reserved.

No part of this publication may be reproduced or used in any form or by any means, electronic or mechanical, including photocopying, recording, or by any information storage and retrieval system, without the express written permission from the copyright owner. For information regarding permission, write to: **kevindfinsonauthor@gmail.com**.

Independently Published. ISBN 979-8-9917564-4-0

# DRAGON SIGN

## Table of Contents

                                                                          Page

Chapter 1: First Day's Dawn .................................... 1

Chapter 2: Up Onto the Mountain ........................... 15

Chapter 3: Dragon Sign .............................................. 33

Chapter 4: The Red Dragon ....................................... 55

Chapter 5: The Blue Dragon ...................................... 63

Chapter 6: The Brown Dragon ................................... 71

Chapter 7: The White Dragon .................................... 81

Chapter 8: Streams of Life ......................................... 91

Chapter 9: The End of Dragons ................................111

# DRAGON SIGN

## CHAPTER 1

## FIRST DAY'S DAWN

The quiet mountain village was still sleepy from its night of rest. Rocky outcroppings surrounding the village looked almost as if a rainbow had been trapped in them. There were shades of faint reds and oranges in some rocks, while there were light tans and darker browns in others. If one looked closely, the hue of a thin layer of bluestone might creep out from between the other colors. The background of rainbow rocks made for a natural piece of artwork as it struck a contrast with the almost-white stones that had been used to make the few dozen houses of the village.

Mountain mist was still settled up in the high mountain valleys above the village. It lazily swirled and flowed as light breezes rumpled it as they descended from the peaks into the crags and valleys. The mist draped itself over the trees covering the mountainside almost like a coat spreading itself over them to protect them from harsh weather. White smoke was beginning to twist its way upward from the chimneys of several of the houses, seeming to reach up toward the mountain mist in hopes of joining it. A street, if one could call it that, wound its way amongst the houses from one end of the village to the other. The street was not paved with stones, but many years of travelers had pressed down the small gravel on it so it was almost like paving. As the street left the village at either end, its pavement-like character gave way to packed dirt with some stones in it. Behind some of the houses were small wooden barns surrounded by rickety wooden fences that once were mountain trees growing where the houses now stood.

It was now the long-awaited morning for Oel. The red and orange rays of the sun were just now peeking above the mountain peaks in the distance. The few clouds in the sky to the east seemed to glow as the sun's beams touched them. Oel sat up in his bed and stared out his bedroom window at the sky as it gradually turned from a dark gray to a reddish orange tinged with blue.

The morning seemed extra fresh this morning in their mountain village. Oel imagined the fresh sunlight embracing their house and then flowing like a slow tide of light that would bring the village out of its slumber and into the new day. The old brown wood around the window framed the image as if it was the artwork of some old master artist. Dust hanging the air caught the early sun's rays and sparkled as it drifted to and fro. It was as if the sun was reaching into Oel's bedroom to gently touch him and awaken him for the day.

Oel's heart was beating with excitement! Today was the day for children in the village to go on "The Walk." It was for children who had reached a certain age. It was a step in becoming an adult. Oel had been looking forward to this since he first learned about "The Walk" in his early childhood years. Like the other children in the village, Oel would be taking "The Walk" with his grandfather. Grandfathers were considered to be the wise men of the village. It was during "The Walk" that they would share some of life's wisdom with the children.

"The Walk" was at least an all-day affair, and could extend to several days in some cases. It always began early in the morning, and often did not end until after the sun had set for the day. Oel had asked Grandfather about "The Walk," but Grandfather would just smile and say that Oel would learn all about it when the time was right. Oel knew that his father and all the other fathers had taken "The Walk", just as did their grandfathers and great grandfathers and all the men that came before them. He also knew that his mother and all the village mothers had taken "The Walk," and it was the same for all the grandmothers and women who had come before, too. And although he never really knew what each of them had experienced on their walks, he knew their experiences had all been different from each other.

It seemed that no one's walk was the same as anyone else's walk. That much he had been able to determine from prying information from his elders. But each person's experiences were deeply personal and not something that was freely discussed. Even so, one could tell something about how those experiences affected people by the way they went about living life on the mountain. Oel's father once told him that what one learns on "The Walk" is unique to the person. What one learns fills that person's needs in certain ways that would not satisfy the needs of someone else. What one learns makes someone the kind of person they will be for the rest of his or her life. Oel was certain that whatever experience he might have on "The Walk" it would be a good one, because it seemed all the men and women in the village were exceptionally good and caring people.

The bed creaked as Oel slid off its side and onto the floor. There wasn't much to the bed. Just some thick wooden boards for the sides and top and bottom ends, and some ropes zig-zagging back and forth between the boards to hold up the mattress. The ropes sometimes had to be pulled and tightened to keep them from sagging too much. The mattress was really just a feather tick made with some cotton cloth sewn together like a giant bag and stuffed with goose feathers. Oel had heard that some folks down in the valleys below filled theirs with corn shucks. He thought feathers were the better of the two. His feather tick was not very thick, and it could get lumps in it at times, but it was better than sleeping on the floor.

The old wooden floor had been worn smooth over the years from the steps of many members of the family who had once had this same bedroom as their own. Oel didn't really know how many people had once had that room as their bedroom, but it had been quite a few. The house was quite old, and so was the family lineage. So, there had been ample time for the floor to become worn. Oel was glad for that. He tried to imagine how rough the floor might have been when it was newer. That would not have been as welcome to one's feet!

Off toward one end of the room he had to be careful where he stepped. Some of the old square nails handmade that were used to fasten down the floor boards had a habit of poking up their heads just enough to catch the bottom of one's foot. Even so, Oel was thankful that he had floorboards in his room. He knew some folks who didn't have a second story in their houses and had packed dirt floors instead of wooden ones.

Oel stood up straight, arched his back and stretched in front of the window. Although there was a chill in the mountain air right now, it had the feeling the day would later become a warm one. So, Oel put on a lightweight shirt and his pants. He figured his outfit might cause him to be a little cool first thing this morning, but it would be more comfortable later in the day as the sun warmed the mountainside. The floorboards gave a soft but welcome groan with each step Oel took as he dressed and then walked out of his bedroom. The old wooden stairs echoed the groans of the floorboards as Oel skipped down them to the lower part of the house.

As he got to the last couple of steps, the fireplace across the room came into view. Some of the early sunbeams were filtering through the kitchen window and touched the fireplace stones, giving them a light yellowish-brown hue. Most of the stones were large, as were the ones that made the walls of the house, but the biggest stone was the long flat one that made up the mantle. It would have taken a strong man to lift those stones, but that mantle stone must have required at least a half dozen men with strong arms and backs to lift it into place. The hearth extended out several feet from the fireplace and was made of large stones that had been flatted on their top sides in an effort to create as level a surface as possible. Many of the hearthstones had been worn smooth, like the wooden floor, with many years of use.

The fireplace's firebox was big and recessed well back beyond the stones fronting the fireplace. The firebox had been constructed so it was deep and could accommodate large pots hanging on hooks that could be swung over the fire for cooking food. A person could just about walk into the firebox without bending down very much! Just above the fireplace opening the stones were stained black from smoke that had escaped through the front instead of through the chimney. That tended to occur when really big fires were kept in the fireplace. Except for very cold winter days, there was usually no need for fires like that.

Oel saw his mother bending over and reaching into the gaping opening of the fireplace to move around a couple of the cast iron pots. She used an iron hook rod to grab one of the swinging hooks and pulled the pot away from the fire and toward her so she could stir something in the pot.

Father and Mother had been up early that morning preparing the things Oel would need for his walk. Father had done both his chores and Oel's. The animals outside in the pens by the barn had been fed and watered. There was a fresh stack of firewood that had been brought into the house and piled next to the fireplace. The stack was made with a mix of large and small logs, and Oel recognized some of them as those he and Father had axed and sawed the week before. Several wooden buckets of fresh well water sat on the floor by the kitchen table where Father had placed them earlier. Their rope handles hung limply over their sides. Father had started the fire in the fireplace so Mother could cook their breakfast, and he now stood watch with an iron poker to stir up the hot coals and cinders and keep the logs burning. Usually, Mother started and tended to the fire and cooked breakfast as Oel did his morning chores outside with Father. But today they were trying to move things along a little bit faster than usual. So, getting an extra early start and sharing tasks was the critical thing for the day's start.

Oel could smell the breakfast his mother had been fixing for the family. The smell tickled his nose! His mouth watered. He was anxious to get started on "The Walk," but knew his mother and father would insist he eat first so he would have the energy to go out into the mountains with Grandfather. Oel thought he already had enough energy, but his tummy rumbled to let him know it was time to eat something. Mother was removing the iron pots from the fireplace and setting them on the wooden kitchen table. With each lid lifted, sumptuous breakfast smells wafted through the kitchen.

Breakfast that morning included some hot biscuits with sweet fruit spread. Having fruit spread was a rarity, so that was something extra special for the morning. Breakfast also included some slices of cooked ham and hot oat mush. Except for the fruit spread, it was the usual breakfast for the day. But today it seemed to have some special quality to it. Oel couldn't quite tell what it was. Maybe it just seemed to have a special feel to it because it was the day of "The Walk" and everything else had a special feel about it.

Steam wafted up from Oel's bowl of mush and twisted and turned as it swirled slowly upward toward his face. He closed his eyes and inhaled the smell slowly and deeply. Father, Mother, Oel and his sister sat down around the kitchen table, bowed their heads and said a morning prayer of thanksgiving for their home, meal, and each other. Breakfast was usually a time of much chatter, but today everyone seemed oddly quiet. Oel could see Father's eyes glancing at him between bites of food, and he could detect a faint smile on his face. Mother's eyes were bright and glistening, and Sister was fidgety like she was sitting on hot coals. Oel could tell she was trying to not ask too many questions about what was going to come that day. Even if she did, Oel would not know what to tell her. She would be taking "The Walk" in a few more years herself, but she was still anxious for Oel about the whole affair.

As everyone was finishing the last bites of their breakfast, there was a knock on the house door. The door was made of thick planks of rough-hewn wood that were accented with knots and gnarly grain. The heavy oak had darkened with age and now had a deep rich brown hue to it. The thickness of the wood made the knock sound like a low, loud thump.

Oel's head shot up from his gaze down at his bowl, and Sister giggled and jumped up and down on her bench. Mother gently touched Sister's arms and softly whispered something to calm her. Father turned his head toward the door, grinned, and then scooted his bench back away from the table so he could stand up and go answer the door. Oel thought Father moved especially quick, yet his movement was almost silent. Even so, before Father could reach the door, there came yet another thump on the wood. Thump, thump, thump!

The iron doorknob groaned and the hinges holding the door to the doorframe creaked softly as Father opened it. That old door protested every time it was opened, but considering its age and all the times it had stood between the family and the weather outside, Oel guessed the door should be allowed to have something to say whenever it was disturbed. Father pulled the door open, slowly at first, and then with almost a flourish at the end. Standing in the middle of the doorway was the silhouette of a large man. The sun behind him was now shining brightly, its rays seeming to bend around him. His face was in the man. The sun behind him was now shining brightly, its rays seeming to bend around him. His face was in the shadow and would be difficult for anyone to recognize. But Oel knew who it was. He knew that figure well. It was Grandfather!

" 'Bout time you got that door opened!" Grandfather said laughingly as he stepped into the house. Father reached out and gave Grandfather a hug, then motioned him further into the house near the kitchen table where everyone could easily see him. He had mountain trousers on and hiking boots made from the leather of a mountain goat he had hunted many years ago. His shirt was forest green in color and seemed to sag off his arms and around his waist. Across his shoulders was a fleece vest, and slung over his shoulder was a satchel and a blanket roll. His large strong hand grasped a walking staff that was almost as long as he was tall. It had been carved from a tree that had been struck by lightning high up on the mountain many years ago. The grain in the staff's wood was twisted and gnarled as if the lightning bolt was still trying to get through it. In his other hand he held his hat. It was broad-rimed with air holes around the top just above the brim. It had been made of the same leather as his boots. It had served him well over the years.

"Would you care to join us for some breakfast?" asked Father.

"Thank you, but no." said Grandfather. "I have

already had my fill of breakfast for the morning. It all smells and looks pretty tasty, but I must decline your generous offer. There is only so much one's stomach can hold!"

Then he turned toward the table and looked straight at Oel.

"Oel," Grandfather said, "Are you ready to get started on your walk? The morning is moving along and so should we."

"He'll be ready in just a couple more minutes," said Mother. "He still needs to pack his satchel with some food to keep him on his way."

"Then he'd best be getting to it!" said Grandfather. "The day's not waiting on us."

Oel jumped up from his bench with a huge grin and ran to grab Grandfather and give him a strong hug. Grandfather patted Oel on his back and tilted his head toward the coat rack next to the door. "Best get your satchel filled, your blanket roll tied . . . and your hat on, Oel" he said. By the time his hug was finished, Mother had already stuffed Oel's satchel with food for his walk and was holding it out to him. She had carefully placed the food parcels inside a heavy cloth shirt that Oel might need in the cooler air up the mountain. Father was also reaching out, holding a filled waterskin. The waterskin had originally been made as a wineskin, but Oel was not allowed to drink wine just yet. Perhaps that would change after "The Walk." Oel took the satchel and waterskin, slung them over his shoulders, and gave a quick hug to Mother, Father, and sister. He then stood up as straight as he could, puffing out his chest and looked into Grandfather's eyes.

"I'm ready, Grandfather!"

With that, Grandfather put his arm around Oel's shoulders and shuffled him out the door. As the two stepped beyond the door threshold, each looked back with a smile and waved at the family watching from the doorway. The adventure, "The Walk," had finally begun.

## CHAPTER 2

## UP ONTO THE MOUNTAIN

It seemed just minutes before Oel and Grandfather had reached the end of the hard road at the edge of the village. Oel's mind was on what was ahead for them for the day, and he scarcely noticed the different houses and fences they passed along the road, or the other children and their grandparents who were starting on their walks. At some points on the village road, it seemed as if all the youngsters and grandparents were gathering together. That was not planned, but was just the result of so many beginning their walks at about the same time of the morning. Some were going in the same direction as Oel and Grandfather, while others were going the opposite way.

There was much chatter between some of them as they walked together along the road as a group, but Oel and Grandfather were quiet as they made their way along it. Since everyone's pace was different, the spacing between pairs of children and grandparents grew larger and larger as the group neared the edge of the village. It wasn't long before the chatter was fading to the point where Oel could tell there was talking but not exactly what was being spoken. Oel looked up at Grandfather, and Grandfather smiled. Grandfather tilted his head forward toward the road, and quietly motioned for them to move along up the mountain road.

Oel and Grandfather were not the first pair to leave the village, but there were many behind them yet to depart. It would not be long until all the pairs had gone on their way and left the village behind. Once out of the village, it seemed everyone had their own direction to go, and Oel found he and Grandfather were suddenly alone on the road. The two walked further without speaking. Oel could hear the crunching of small pebbles beneath his feet as he took each step. The light breeze was rustling the leaves on the trees to either side of the road, and there was the occasional song of birds and the scittering of tiny animals as they scampered behind or up into the trees.

Oel had been on the road just outside the village many times. He had been sent to collect berries when they were in season, and knew where the nut tree groves were located. There had also been times when he and Father went out to cut trees for firewood. Most of his trips beyond the village boundaries had kept him close to the stone houses, but once in a while he would go exploring the mountain forest and venture just far enough that the village was not in sight. He and Grandfather walked along steadily, neither slow nor fast, and soon they had reached the part of the forest where Oel had not yet gone.

"How are you doing, Oel?" asked Grandfather.

"I'm fine! Do we go further?" replied Oel.

"Yes, we will go further. Much further. But it has been a couple of hours since we left home, and it is time to stop for a brief rest and have a drink of water." Grandfather said.

Oel replied, "I am not really that thirsty!"

And Grandfather said, "It is important to take frequent drinks of water, especially as we go higher up onto the mountain. You may not feel thirsty right now, but your body will need something to drink much more often than you realize. The path we will be taking will begin to task us. So, drink just a little bit now . . . before we continue on our walk."

The two sat down side-by-side with their backs against a towering pine tree. Each opened his waterskin and sipped a little water. They sat in silence, listening to the forest.

"What are you listening for, Grandfather?" asked Oel.

"I'm listening to the forest. I'm listening to it speaking to us." replied Grandfather.

"I don't hear it, Grandfather. What is it saying?" asked Oel.

"It is speaking about life, Oel. It is speaking about the wonderful things God created and put here."

Oel said, "Oh! I still don't hear the forest saying

those things."

Grandfather explained. "The forest does not speak to us in words like we use. It has its own language – or many languages. I think you have heard them before, but just did not realize what you were hearing. It is important to learn to listen to the language of the forest so you can let it guide you and protect you. It is important to listen to what the forest tells you. It can tell you when everything is okay, and when you should be alert for trouble. It can tell you when things are healthy and good, and when they are not."

"How can the forest protect us, Grandfather?" asked Oel.

"The forest can give us shelter, and food. The forest provides us with trees for our homes, fruits, nuts, and animals to eat. It can shield us from the harshest winter winds, and from the summer's burning heat. It gives us the fresh air that we breathe, and it keeps the waters flowing in the streams pure and cool." explained Grandfather.

"Can the forest tell us other things, Grandfather?" queried Oel.

"Yes, it can. It can tell us about its past, and our past as people. It can tell us about what is coming in its future, and our future, too." Answered Grandfather. "There are signs the forest gives that speaks those things to us."

"Grandfather, what are those signs?" asked Oel.

"You will learn some of them as we continue on our walk, Oel." said Grandfather. "But for now, look past the old road and into the trees just beyond. What is it you see, Oel?"

Oel squinted his eyes a little and peered out into the forest. "I see a lot of trees, Grandfather."

"What is it you see about the trees?" asked Grandfather.

"They are tall and have a lot of leaves on them." answered Oel.

"What else?" pressed Grandfather.

"Well, I see birds up in their branches, and nests, and squirrels sitting in them." said Oel.

"And what about the trees themselves?" continued Grandfather. "Do they look healthy, do they look sick and sad? How do they look, Oel?"

"Hmmm." said Oel. "They seem to be healthy. Their bark is good, and they have a lot of branches and the leaves on them are a nice dark green."

"Yes," said Grandfather. "The trees are telling us they are healthy. But that is not always the case. When we see trees with bark that is falling off, or leaves that are curling and turning brown when it is not autumn, then we know there is something amiss. The trees are telling us they are having trouble. If it is just a single tree, that is not so much a worry. But if it is a number of trees, then we should pay close attention to what is happening. We should start looking for those things that might be harming the trees. The trees keep the forest healthy, and if the trees are sick, then the forest is sick. And a sick forest means we will have troubles living here. It can mean we will have fewer berries and nuts to find for food. It means we may have trouble finding the animals we rely upon for meat and skins. When the trees are healthy, all those things thrive. When the trees are sick, all things suffer."

"Oh, I see." said Oel.

"We also need to understand how to help the forest stay healthy." said Grandfather. "We must use it judiciously."

"What does that mean?" asked Oel.

Grandfather said, "It means we must only take from the forest what we really need. If we take too much, like cutting down too many trees or killing too many animals, then the forest suffers. It has trouble recovering and staying healthy. And, there are times when we don't take enough from it. If we don't take enough animals for our use, then there become too many of them for the forest to support. It's like when there are too many rabbits and they overrun everything and destroy the berries and plants that the other animals – and we – rely on. We must be good stewards of the forest and our world. That is a responsibility God has given to us."

"Are there other signs the forest uses to speak to us, Grandfather? What are they?"

Grandfather sighed softly. "Yes, there are many other signs. We can listen to the way the wind moves through the forest. Trees and bushes with healthy branches and leaves have one kind of sound while unhealthy ones have a different sound. The soil itself can tell us things, too. It should have a certain color and smell to it, depending on where you are in the forest. The rocks tell us things, such as what the weather has been like. Some wear down in certain ways depending on what the weather has done to them over the years. You would not want to build your house where the rocks show much wear because of harsh winds and rains. The moss on the trees and rocks also tells us things. The thicker and deeper green it is, the healthier it is, and the better the moisture in the forest."

"Then, there are the animals." Grandfather bent down and pointed to the ground. He stretched out his index finger and lightly touched a track in the soil. Oel would not have seen it had Grandfather not pointed it out. As if tracks began jumping up out of the ground, Oel began seeing more of them. They formed a wandering line going between the trees. Then there was another set of tracks alongside the first.

"See that? This set of tracks was made by a small animal, probably a rabbit by the looks of it. And that other set of tracks was made by a larger animal, probably a wolf. See how the toes dig a little deeper into the soil and are far apart? That means the larger animal was hurrying, probably to catch that rabbit for its dinner. The animals all have behaviors that are particular to them, like the wolf hunting the rabbit for food. When they behave normally, as we expect them to do, then the forest is healthy. But when animals begin to behave oddly, then there are troubles coming that we need to watch for."

Oel bent down and touched the tracks with his fingers. Then he looked back to see what kinds of tracks he had left. He pointed to them and said, "Look, Grandfather! I left tracks, too!"

Grandfather nodded. "Yes, and not only in the soil. Your feet have left marks on the rocks wherever you stepped on them. Wherever you passed, you left cracked branches on the ground, or shuffled leaves to expose the ground. You also bent the stems of plants as you passed by them. Wherever you touched the trees, your hands have moved the moss that might have been growing on them. You have left all kinds of tracks behind you. If you know how to read tracks, you can follow and find almost anything or anyone. And once you know that, you can travel in ways that leave few tracks behind."

Oel grinned and said, "I guess that would be handy if you didn't want someone to follow and find you!"

Grandfather agreed. Then he said, "But always remember there is someone who will always find you. He will always know exactly where you are."

Oel asked, "Who can do that? How could he know?"

Grandfather said, "It is God. You can never be hidden from Him, or get away from Him. No matter what you do. So, it is always best to try to live the way God wants you to live, because He sees everything. He can see what is in your heart, even if you don't say anything about it."

"I try to be good!" said Oel. "I try to do what is right."

"I know you do." said Grandfather. But there are people who forget that and then do things that are harmful to themselves, or to other people, or to the forest. One person doing one wrong thing can harm all the rest of us, even if they didn't intend it. We people are not perfect, and there are times when each of us will do what is wrong. When we realize we have done that, we need to make amends for it. But I think a very important thing for you to understand is that God will forgive each of us for the wrongs we commit, especially if we ask Him for forgiveness."

Oel stood up and brushed the dirt off his fingers. "That dirt was musty!"

Grandfather said, "Yes, there is a smell to the forest. The soil has its own smell, and even the rocks have theirs. So do the trees and plants, and each kind of animal. A healthy forest has a cool, fresh smell to it. It is the kind of smell you want to stand and inhale as deeply as possible."

Oel closed his eyes and inhaled deeply. Then, he reached down and dug his fingers into the soil at the base of the tree. He glanced up along the trunk of the tree to look at its bark. He stood up and slowly walked around the tree looking at the moss growing on it.

"Well, enough break!" said Grandfather. "It is time to move along!"

Oel and Grandfather slung their waterskins, satchels, and blanket rolls over their shoulders and started walking again. Oel listened more carefully to things around them as they walked. He tried to listen for the wind in the trees and the movement of the animals nearby. He inhaled more deeply and more frequently to try smelling the forest. Before he realized it, Grandfather had stopped and turned toward him.

"This is where we leave the old road," he said.

"Where are we going?" asked Oel.

Grandfather pointed up into the trees off to the side of the road. "We are going up there!"

Oel looked up into the trees. There was no road there. There was not even a path. It looked like rough going. The mountain slope looked steep in places, and there were some rocky ledges reaching out from the mountainside as if they were trying to grab for some sunlight. Rocks of different sizes were strewn between the trees, and there were ruts and cuts in the soil and rocks from the runoff of rains. There were dead tree branches criss-crossing the way between some trees. Oel wasn't sure he wanted to go that way.

"Up through that!?" asked Oel, wrinkling his brow.

"Yes," said Grandfather. "Up there. We have far to go. And it is important that we go where few other people have gone. There is something up there that the forest and mountain want us to learn. There is something there that God wants us to understand. We can't do that down here."

"Down here!" thought Oel. They had been walking the road all that time, going up and up higher into the mountain. They were much higher than where the village was. He wondered how much higher they were going to go. "Grandfather, how far is it we need to go?"

"Almost to the top of the mountain." Replied Grandfather. "Almost to the top."

"Is that where God will tell us what He wants us to understand?" asked Oel.

"That is one place where He will reveal things to us." said Grandfather. "But He will also reveal things to us as we make our way up to the top. Part of our learning is what comes to us along the journey, and part is what we get once we arrive at our destination. Both are important. We must not think one is more important than the other. And there will likely be more learning on our way back home."

Oel was starting to feel tired. And thinking about getting up the mountainside made him feel even more tired. His legs were becoming a little weak and his steps less sure. His back was starting to ache from the satchel, waterskin, and blanket roll, and from leaning forward as he trekked up and up onto the mountainside. Once in a while, his foot would slip and he would slide backward a foot or two. His climbing staff was wearing tender spots on his hand. There was a faint hint of a headache building up inside his head. Oel wondered if Grandfather was getting tired yet, too. Grandfather did not seem to be looking weak or having much trouble walking onward.

Grandfather stopped and turned toward Oel. He reached out his hand for Oel to grab, and then pulled Oel up their path a little further. "Not much further for today, Oel." said Grandfather. He pointed to what looked like a rock ledge not far above them. "That," said Grandfather, "is where we will stop and rest and eat."

It seemed to Oel that it took about as long to get up to that rock ledge as it had taken them to walk all the way up that old road from the village. Grandfather was the first to step up onto the ledge, and he helped pull Oel up to be beside him. Oel brushed the dirt off his knees and arms, and slowly straightened his back.

As Oel stood straight, he looked down and out across the mountain. He almost gasped! The view before him was more beautiful than anything he could have imagined. He could see the tops of so many of the trees he and Grandfather had passed earlier in the day. The green was punctuated by dark gray shadows and light brown patches peeking out from the ground between the trees. A mist was starting to form down below them, encircling the very tops of the trees as if it was gently laying a blanket on them.

Far beyond, Oel could make out the shapes of other mountains and the valleys between them. The sun was no longer shining in the valleys, and he could see them gradually get darker as the mountain shadows of the early evening crept into them. Things seemed strangely quiet. It was the time for the change of day between when day animals stopped their roaming and the night creatures arose to take their tours of the mountain. A breeze wisped across Oel's face, brushing his hair gently. It was cool. Much cooler than the breezes he felt all day long. There was a chill to it, but not really cold. In a way, it was the most refreshing part of the whole day!

"Quite a feeling, isn't it?" asked Grandfather as he took in a long, deep breath and stood as tall and straight as he could.

Oel continued standing on the rock ledge silently looking out over the scene.

"It's much more than just what one can see. It is something that impresses itself into your heart." said Grandfather. "It is something that will settle itself into your mind, and nothing else you will ever see will seem quite the same."

Oel replied in a very soft whisper almost impossible to hear. "Yes. Yes, it is!"

Grandfather gently tugged on Oel's arm and nudged him away from the rock ledge edge and closer to the mountainside. They opened their satchels and unrolled their blankets, and then removed some food. Oel had forgotten how hungry he had been. He had forgotten how tired he felt just a few minutes earlier on their climb. He and Grandfather said a prayer, and in the quiet of the early mountain evening ate their meal together. It was the first meal Oel would ever have up on the mountain beyond the village. It was a very special meal.

Grandfather gathered a few twigs and small branches that were scattered along the rock ledge and started a fire. It was not a large fire . . . just enough to give them a little warmth.

By then, the sun had set and the quiet darkness wrapped itself around Oel and Grandfather like a blanket. It seemed to Oel the darkness was almost suffocating, but at the same time was fresh and invigorating. He inhaled deeply to try breathing it in. It was as if the night mountain air was renewing him in some way. The moon had just peeked above the horizon, and its light cast shadows off the rocks and trees below, making them seem almost as if they were moving with a life of their own.

Oel listened to his breathing and thought he could hear his heart beating. Through the quiet of the night, he could hear the sounds of the night animals as they rustled their way amongst the trees. Once in a while there was the soft scratch of something on tree bark or rock, and a few times a nearly-silent whimper of a small animal. A distant owl hooted, and was quiet for a short while before hooting again. The air was still except for an occasional puff of breeze that glided down the mountainside above. It was barely enough to rustle the leaves in the trees. Oel wondered if he was actually hearing that or just imagining it.

Oel leaned back, folded his arms behind his head, and looked upward. The sky was brilliantly dark. There seemed to be far more stars than Oel had ever thought existed. They twinkled brightly and some seemed to be trying to hide behind light dusty finger-like whisps that stretched from one end of the sky to the other. Oel imagined he could hear the twinkle of the stars as if they were glass crystals clinking softly together. Oel had, of course, seen stars from home back down in the village. But they never were as bright as they were up on the mountain this night.

Grandfather spoke softly. "Can you see the patterns in the stars?"

Oel gazed intently upward. "I can see some. I see the big bear and the small bear. There are a couple of others I see, too. And there is the North Star." Oel pointed to the northern part of the sky.

Grandfather nodded. "People can see different patterns and shapes in the stars. It kind of depends upon where they live and grew up. What you see as the big bear might look like something else to someone living distant lands. But whatever the pattern is for a group of stars, it has meaning and it has a use for us. God created our world and then put all those stars up there for us to see. I sometimes think He created the stars in order to decorate our world down here. I know of men who sail on the seas who rely on those shapes to tell them where they are when out on their ships and cannot see any land. We can use them on land to guide our way during the night, too. Over thousands of years, people made up stories about some of the star patterns. If you look up over there, you will see the Great Hunter. Those few stars in a row are like his belt, and those other stars hanging down from the belt are like his sword. Just above his belt you can see other stars that look like the edges of his shoulders. The Great Hunter moves across the sky as our seasons change. In the summer, he is high in the sky, and in the winter, he is low . . . almost to the horizon. If we watch the movement of the star patterns, we can tell something about the changes of the seasons that are approaching and prepare ourselves for them. It is like a timepiece. God created it that way to help us through the year. I think one of God's most helpful creations was the North Star. You can always see it, no matter where you might be in our land. If you see it, you can use it to guide you on your journeys. It is always in the same place. It is constant, steady, and never changes . . . just like God."

Night had fully arrived, and the time was getting late. Oel and Grandfather wrapped themselves in their blankets, leaned together, and then leaned back against the mountainside. Together, they said their evening prayers, taking turns in sharing their thanksgivings.

Afterward both sat quietly, looking out at the night sky. The night insects were singing, and an owl or two chimed in here and there as if trying to bring some order to the noise. It was a symphony to accompany the show above them. Oel didn't know when, but at some point while looking at the stars he slipped off into sleep.

## CHAPTER 3

## DRAGON SIGN

Oel awoke early the next morning. In his sleep just before waking, he was feeling cold and had curled his legs up to his chest and tightened his blanket around him. When he opened his eyes, he caught a glimpse of the sun's rays poking above the mountain peaks on the horizon just before the sun showed itself. It was pre-dawn, and the air had cooled during the night and was awaiting the warming beams of the sun.

Grandfather had been awake and up just a few minutes earlier, and was busy trying to start a small fire with which they could warm themselves before breakfast. He cupped his hands near his mouth and blew warm air over them to get his fingers limbered up for the task. Oel tucked his blanket a little more tightly around his neck and scooted over to the small fire. He was just barely warm enough to not shiver. Oel and Grandfather bowed their heads and said a morning prayer and blessing for their meal. As they ate their cold breakfast, they listened to the morning calls of birds in the forest below them. Animals were stirring, and their sounds of clacking in the tree branches and rustling the underbrush drifted up to the rock ledge where Oel and Grandfather sat. The forest was waking up. A breeze suddenly puffed up their blankets, and it seemed to Oel that the forest air was waking up, too.

As soon as they finished eating, Oel and Grandfather quickly prepared to continue their walk. Oel looked behind him . . . and the mountain was still there, beckoning them upward. He stretched, trying to loosen his muscles that were still a little stiff from the previous day's climb. When he saw Grandfather stretching in the same way, he didn't feel so bad about his muscle aches. He laughed when Grandfather said he was a little creaky that morning and that his old bones just were not as forgiving as they were when he was younger.

Soon, their satchels were repacked and blanket rolls tied, ready for the day's journey. The sun had risen over the distant mountains and its rays were igniting the sky with reds and oranges. There was enough light now to illuminate the pathway Oel and Grandfather would be taking up the mountainside.

"Well," said Grandfather, "today we go to the summit!"

Oel looked upslope. The mountainside looked rockier than the day before, and there were fewer trees upslope from them. What trees were there were certainly smaller and spaced more widely than the trees below. Oel thought he could pick out the point where trees were no longer able to be growing. It was the tree line, and it was much higher from where they were on the rock ledge. "No vegetation above the tree line," he thought. It looked like the mountaintop would be a cold, harsh place. He wondered why Grandfather had selected that as the place for them to go.

There was no path for them to follow this high up on the mountain. Most of the animal paths were down below. So Oel and Grandfather would have to forge their own way upward. Oel had never scaled a rocky mountain slope before, so he would have to rely on Grandfather's skills finding the footholds and hand placements among the rocks as they worked their way to the summit. The going was slow, and Grandfather knew they would need to take frequent pauses to let their arms and legs rest. At their first stop, they found a boulder to sit on that faced outward and gave a grand view over the expanse past the mountain. Oel was startled by the sudden scitter of a ground squirrel as it dashed past them from one rock to the next. He smiled, and then was startled again when a hawk flew by a little too close, probably searching for the squirrel. Even though the upper part of the mountain looked barren from below at the rock ledge, it wasn't absent life.

Grandfather smiled. "Even in the harshest parts of the world there is life. God made sure life would be everywhere. We sometimes just need to learn how to look for it, and then what to look for. Sometimes, it isn't at all what you expect. The world is full of God's surprises!"

Oel said, "Well, that really surprised me!" as he took a deep breath and looked around for the ground squirrel and hawk.

"It's good to get surprised once in a while!" said Grandfather with a soft laugh. "Keeps us on our toes!"

"I didn't see any sign that the ground squirrel lived here. I just thought there'd be rocks up here." Said Oel.

Grandfather replied, "Sometimes, seeing the signs is more difficult in some places than others, but they are there if you know what to look for. That ground squirrel probably has a small burrow up here between the rocks somewhere. It would look like a small hole with some pebbles pushed up around its entrance. It would look a lot like the rest of the rock pile and outcroppings around it. The ground squirrel makes it burrow that way as protection."

"I see!" said Oel. "I don't think that hawk could get down into that burrow!"

"Even so," said Grandfather, "there are other things the ground squirrel needs to be wary of. It may be safe from the hawk when in its burrow, but there are snakes that can crawl into it and get to the squirrel. The squirrel needs to have a way to avoid those snakes. It might have a second entrance to the burrow it can use as an escape, or it might have to find a strategy for moving and keeping its distance from the snake. You see, Oel, our lives are a lot like that of the ground squirrel. We have our homes and ways of living, and we usually learn to avoid those things that can pose dangers to us. But there are times and circumstances when those dangers come anyway. We cannot avoid them. It is at those times when we must have something else to rely on, like the squirrel relies on another escape route or its movement strategies. An important thing to always remember is that the dangers to come are not always in our physical world. Certainly, there are fires and storms, floods and illnesses, and other such things that come. Those are all physical things. But we also face dangers from spiritual things. If we are not aware of our spiritual world, then we can be harmed by evil that hides there. It will stalk us, just like the hawk stalked the ground squirrel. It sets out to harm and kill our souls. We cannot run and hide from those evils of the spiritual world. We must face them. And we often need help to protect us from them. God offers us that protection. We must have faith that He will send us help. We must use the weapons God has given us to fight those dark evils."

Oel scrunched his eyebrows and nose. Then he asked,

"What weapons, Grandfather?" Oel's face had an expression of puzzlement.

"There are a number of weapons at your disposal, if you just choose to recognize them and use them." Grandfather said.

"Oh, I want to know what they are and how to use them!" Oel exclaimed as he nodded his head up and down vigorously.

"You already have them, Oel. But you may not have recognized what they are or their power. One of them is a strong faith. Always believe that God is there with you, watching out for you. Keep firm in your faith that God will deliver you from evil and oppression of the dark forces. In a similar way, the name of Jesus, God's Son, is a very powerful weapon. God has given each of us the authority to use Jesus' name in our fight against evil. Nothing evil can stand before Jesus or His name. His blood is also a terribly powerful weapon. We share in His body and blood when we partake of communion in church. We should do that often. Doing so strengthens us and helps us remain healthy in spiritual ways. Also, always know who you are, a child of God, and to whom you belong. You belong to God and Jesus. Be steadfast in that knowledge, and it will be an awesome weapon in your arsenal."

Oel said, "I always thought I belonged to Father and

Mother. And to my family."

Grandfather smiled. "Yes, you do. But you, and Father and Mother and all of us, belong to the family of God. We are His children. He will protect His children even more than a she-bear will protect her cubs!"

"It's nice that our family is so big!" exclaimed Oel.

Grandfather continued. "And prayer is very important. Prayer is a powerful weapon. We must pray for help and guidance, and we must also pray to thank God for the good things He blesses us with. I think it important to pray for even the tiniest of things, like the beauty of the sunrise this morning, or the morning song of the birds."

"And the insects singing at night, and the stars in the sky?" asked Oel.

"Yes," Grandfather replied. "Those and many other things. God created them, big and small, weak and strong, bright and dim. And He gave them to us to make our lives better and live in harmony with His creation."

Oel pursed his lips. "I guess I need to pray more about more things. There are so many things."

"Almost everything." said Grandfather. "And there are other weapons you need to know about. Going regularly to worship with the community of others is a weapon we have been given. Members of the community support and help each other, and pray for each other.

That is a strength other communities do not have. Another weapon is scripture. Read the *Bible*, learn from what it shares with you. It is the word of God. It will help you follow the path of life God intends for you to follow. There will be times when you need help understanding scripture, so don't hesitate to ask someone to help you. Your parents, other elders, and our church pastor are good people to seek out at those times. With this weapon comes choosing to do right when it seems easier to do wrong, and helping someone else even though it causes you inconvenience or pain. God's son gave His life through unimaginable pain in order to save us from our sins and the wrongs we have done. It would have been easier for Him to do something else, but He choose to follow God's path for Him and did what was right."

Oel said, "That's sad and wonderful at the same time."

Grandfather replied, "Yes, and sometimes what seems so bad and sad is really what is best and most good. Without knowing what God and Jesus teach us, and failing to understand those things, we are not likely to see the good that comes from the bad. That can cause us to lose hope, and we must hope in the Lord always."

"But I don't want to do bad things, I want to do good things." said Oel with a pout.

"Of course, you do." said Grandfather. "But there will be times in your life when the choices you face look bad to you, and you must pick the ones that help others more than yourself. And those choices may be about big things, or even little things. Think about how your mother sacrifices for you every morning by getting up so early to have your breakfast ready for you when you get up for the day. She does that even when she had been up late the night before. I think she has times when she would much rather stay in bed and rest, but she gets up to do good for you and the family. It may seem like a little thing to you, but it is really not so little when you look at it as God and Jesus want you to see it. So, it is important to respect her and others who give of themselves so your life is better."

"I do respect Mother, and Father, too! And you and Grandmother! I think I should tell all of you that more often. I see how important that is." said Oel.

"So is respecting God's creation and doing our best to be good stewards of it. And the most important weapon is love. Our love for God and His Son – and the love They send to us -- can give us the best protection we can imagine. Their love comes to us through the Holy Spirit, who can fill us with that love. We must always do our utmost to love other people, too. It is easy to love our families, but it is difficult to love people that we find offensive. Evil cannot stand in the face of God's love or overcome the Holy Spirit."

Oel frowned. "I really do not like Fredrick back in our village. He always is mean to me and tries to get me into trouble. Loving him will be very hard, Grandfather!"

Grandfather smiled. "Yes, I know. I had my own Fredrick when I was your age. His name was Francis. I have the same problem with some other folks in the village. But I try my best to treat them kindly and not retaliate when they do wrong to me. It is hard, and there times when I fail. When I fail, I ask God and Jesus to forgive me and help me, to guide me through the situation, and heal the wounds we have inflicted upon one another. You see, the problems that exist like that come from evil, and it is only through the love of God and Jesus, through the help of the Holy Spirit, that we can push that evil out and live better lives."

Oel sighed deeply. "I see. I will try from now on to do better. Sometimes, it feels good to punch Fredrick, but I know that is wrong. And it really doesn't help anything get better. He just comes back another time and does something else to me."

Grandfather nodded his head. "Yes. It will be a challenge for you. But I think you can do it. Maybe after a while Fredrick will stop being mean to you and both of you can live in peace with one another. Francis and I are now friends, so I know it can happen."

"I hope so!" said Oel. "I hope so."

The two sat on the boulder a short time longer, and then Grandfather stood up and waived his arm up at the mountain. He pointed with is walking staff. "Time to move on!" he said.

With that, they resumed their trek up the mountainside. By now, the sun was high in the sky and was baking the ground. To Oel, the sunlight seemed much brighter than usual, and he had to squint his eyes to deal with it. They were now high enough on the mountain that the only sounds coming to them were made by the wind passing by them. The summit of the mountain was almost within reach. Maybe just another half hour of hiking would get them there. It would be nearly noon when they arrived – just in time for lunch!

Finally, Oel and Grandfather stepped onto the mountain's summit. Grandfather stood as tall as he could, and Oel slumped and wiped the perspiration off his brow. Then, Grandfather grabbed Oel's hand and raised their arms over their heads as if victorious from a long contest. Both breathed deeply. "Time for lunch!" said Grandfather as he allowed their arms to drop.

"I am so ready!" said Oel.

Lunch seemed to taste extra good that day. Oel ate

slowly and savored each bite. The flavors seemed so much better than he remembered when eating the same things down at home. The breeze at the summit seemed constant and helped keep him cool even though he was sitting out in the bright sunlight. He was not in a hurry to finish his lunch. As he chewed the last bite, he again started to wonder why Grandfather had brought them up to the top of the mountain.

"Grandfather, why did you choose to come here, to the top of the mountain?" asked Oel.

"Because I want you to see some things that you can't see from anywhere else." replied Grandfather. "It is time you see them and understand things about them."

Then, Grandfather raised his arm and pointed his walking staff to another mountain off in the distance to the south. "I want you to look at that mountain. It is called Pyrope Peak. Look at it and tell me what you see."

Oel shielded his eyes with his hand, squinted his eyes, and looked at the mountain Grandfather was pointing toward. While he did so, he asked, "What does Pyrope mean, Grandfather?"

"It comes from the Greek language. It means 'fiery-eyed'" answered Grandfather.

The longer Oel looked at Pyrope Peak, the more he could see it had a color different than other peaks around it. It was darker. There were large portions of the peak that were black. Green was scarce on its slopes. It did not look like a welcoming place to be.

"Why is it so black, Grandfather?" asked Oel.

"It is black because of fire. It has been burned. It did not burn because of what usually causes forest fires. It is dragon sign" replied Grandfather.

Oel frowned. "Dragon sign? What does that mean?"

There was a sternness in Grandfather's voice that Oel had not heard before. It was almost startling to hear that tone in his voice. "It means it is the sign that a dragon was there," said Grandfather. He pursed his lips and took in a slow, deep breath.

"A dragon! I didn't think dragons were real" Oel blurted out.

Then Grandfather turned slightly to the west and pointed to another place. He pointed his walking staff to a deep valley between two mountains. The valley was filled by a deep lake. The lake seemed to extend far to the horizon. "Oel," he said, "what do you see over there?"

"I see a lake down in that valley, Grandfather. It looks like a very big lake!" said Oel.

"That is Nilakanta Lake" said Grandfather. "Nilakanta means 'blue-throated'. Nilakanta Lake starts down there and reaches all the way to the sea past the horizon. It would take us many days to walk there."

"Funny," said Oel, "the nearer end of the lake looks calm and still, but farther out it looks rough with high waves and dark stormy clouds. I don't think boats would want to be there!"

"That, too, is dragon sign." said Grandfather.

Grandfather turned a little further and pointed northward to yet another place. "Look there, Oel. What do you see there?"

Oel looked, and Grandfather was pointing his walking staff to yet another mountain peak to the north.

"Over there is Petrous Point." said Grandfather.

The mountain seemed to Oel to be surrounded by multiple stone walls. There looked like one surrounding the base of the mountain, another about a fourth of the way up the mountainside, a third further up, with yet a fourth surrounding its summit. Oel could tell the walls were made of stone because their size was so large their edges could be easily seen from where he stood. He also could tell the stone walls were very tall, at least six men high, and very thick. Oel wondered how any men could have built such a thing. There did not appear to be any gates or spaces in any of the walls. Whatever was outside the walls would be kept out, and whatever was inside the walls would be kept in. The mountainside was mainly a brown color with some small scrub brush scattered here and there. Nestled into the brown were dark places that looked like holes, or caves. Oel told Grandfather what he thought he was seeing.

"That is exactly what you are seeing, and it is also dragon sign, Oel. 'Petrous' means 'resembling rock or stone' and what you see over there may be harder than any stone you know of that exists anywhere else." said Grandfather.

Just then, the flash of the sun caught Oel's eye. It came from somewhere off to his right side toward the south. He turned around in time to see yet another flash in the east. The brightness made Oel quickly close his eyes and cover them with his hands as if to protect them.

"What was that?!" he exclaimed.

"That is the fourth dragon sign." said Grandfather. "When you can, look at the clouds around that mountain over there. The mountain is Brenna Palisade. 'Brenna' means 'blazing light.' What can you see there?"

Oel strained his eyes. "A lot of blazing!" He grimaced a little. "The mountain seems to glisten, Grandfather. It looks like a long row of very high cliffs that are sparkly. The sunlight seems to jump off them. It reminds me of shining crystals. The clouds around the cliffs glisten, too! It is hard to look at!" Oel closed his eyes to give them a rest from the brightness.

Grandfather nodded his head up and down in agreement. "That is the palisade. It is important for you to understand those dragon signs, Oel. There are lessons to be learned from what they mean."

"Grandfather, where did the dragons come from? Are they still here?" asked Oel.

"Nobody knows for sure where the dragons came from. There is a legend, though, that speaks about it. Legends may or may not be true, but I think there is some truth hidden within them."

"So, what does the legend say, Grandfather?" Oel sat down, crossed his legs, put his elbows on his knees, and propped his chin with his hands. He tilted his head to the side slightly, giving emphasis to his question.

Grandfather began the tale. "Legend says the dragons were created by God. When God had created the earth, the seas, and the sky, He then turned to creating the creatures to live in those places. He created angels and then began creating animals. Some of the first God created were dragons. They were magnificent creatures. No other animal would be as large. No other animal would have all the different skills and abilities that the dragons would have. They were not equal to the angels, but they were powerful and intelligent creatures nonetheless.

The first one God created was a beautiful one He named Lucifer. Some people know Lucifer by other names, or by other forms such as the serpent or the snake.

As with all His creatures, God gave Lucifer free will, the ability to choose. Lucifer became jealous of God and His creations, and decided he wanted them for himself. His jealously became so great that it darkened his entire heart, and then all of his body. He became darker than the darkest of night. It warped him and gnarled him until his once beautiful body was horribly ugly and twisted and frightful. Lucifer became rebellious against God and the angels who obeyed Him. But God allowed Lucifer to remain with Him in heaven until Lucifer decided to put himself above God and take everything for himself. He convinced some of the angels to join him. That is when God cast Lucifer and the other rebellious angels out of heaven.

"The second dragon God created was red in color like the fire God drew from to make the sun and the stars. The third one He created was a blue one, like the color of the waters with which He filled the basins of the earth. It was the color of the earth's waters, the lakes and rivers and seas. Then God created the fourth dragon, and it was brown in color like the soil and rocks that God made when forming the solid earth. Finally, God created the fifth dragon, and it was brilliant crystal white just like diamonds. That dragon's color was like the clouds of the sky, the ice and snow of mountain glaciers, and the wisp of the wind."

Oel asked, "Did God make other dragons?"

Grandfather said, "I do not know. The legend only speaks about those five. I think other dragons that people in the world talk about are different versions of those last four. People have given those different versions different names. So that can be confusing to us."

"Is that all the legend says?" asked Oel.

"No, there is more." replied Grandfather. "All of God's creations were pure and clean. The same was true for the last four dragons. But Lucifer had other designs on God' creations. Lucifer wanted to take control of what God had created, and if he couldn't control it, he wanted to ruin or destroy it. God found out about Lucifer's evil ways and cast him out of heaven. But before that happened, Lucifer placed a poison in each of the last four dragons. He took his finger and reached into the breast of each of the four last dragons and touched their hearts. With that touch, he implanted a spot of darkness into them. Then, those dark spots opened the dragons to the possibility of ignoring God's wishes. It introduced to them a rebelliousness. Each time any of the dragons wanted to ignore God's wishes and rebel a little bit, its dark spot on its heart would grow just a little bit larger.

"There was still a lot of good in each dragon's heart, but that dark spot was a cancer that constantly tugged on the dragon's willingness to do as God wanted. So, there existed in each dragon a battle between the good part of their hearts and the darkness Lucifer had implanted within them. Lucifer hoped that darkness would grow and grow until it overtook all the goodness in the dragons' hearts, and the dragons would be lost to God forever. After God had cast Lucifer and the other rebellious angels out of heaven, He saw the damage that Lucifer had inflicted on the four dragons. They were no longer pure. And not being pure, they could not remain in heaven. So, God sent the dragons to live on the earth. Once sent down, each dragon claimed a part of the earth to tend to it."

"So, are any of those dragons still here?" queried Oel.

"That is hard to say." answered Grandfather. "I am not sure the dragons are here in the same form as they were when they were first put on the earth. But I do think they are still here in different forms. It is those different forms that impact the world and all people, and that we can see as dragon sign."

Oel pondered all that Grandfather had told him about the legend of where the dragons came from. He sat quietly staring off at the different mountains on the distant horizon, and at the lake nestled between two of them. He did not know how long he was thinking about it all, but suddenly found himself being shaken by

Grandfather. The sun was well on its journey toward late afternoon, and it was time Oel and Grandfather started on their way down the mountain. They could not spend the night at the summit. It would be much too cold, and they were not prepared for that. The goal was to reach the rock ledge partway down the mountainside where they had spent their first night. Going down would be faster than the trek up, but considering where the sun was in its trip across the sky, getting to the rock ledge would be about as far as they could go before darkness descended upon them and hide the path downward. It would not be safe traversing the side of the mountain after dark.

On their way down, Oel tried to find the boulder where they had rested next to the ground squirrel earlier. But Grandfather was evidently leading them in a slightly different path and Oel did not see the boulder. He settled for looking around for ground squirrels skittering among the rocks. That familiar hawk was circling high in the air, ready to pounce down on its supper.

The air seemed to get a little warmer as Oel and Grandfather made their way down the slope. Soon, the bare rocks began to give way to some small plants, and then to scrawny trees. They had reached the tree line. Oel felt somehow relieved that they had reached that point on the mountainside. It meant the rock ledge was not that much farther downslope. Although going downslope was faster that going up, it seemed to be taking more of a toll on his muscles as they stretched and tensed to keep him from stumbling and falling down head over heels. A few missteps caused some smaller rocks to rumble and tumble down in front of them, and Oel did not want to be rolling downward like them. And, his stomach was starting to rumble. It was calling him to feed it.

"Here we are!" shouted Grandfather as they finally stepped on the rock ledge. He let out a big sigh of relief. The sun had not yet set, and the light was good enough to see details of the rock outcrop. Grandfather found a small niche in the mountainside that would give them a little more cover and protection from the cold air through the night. The first night they had not seen the niche. He had Oel help gather some twigs and branches for a fire, and soon had it burning. Even though it was not yet dark, the warmth from the fire felt welcome. The two sat down near the fire, bowed their heads, and said some prayers thanking God for a safe trip up to the summit and back, and for the food they were about to eat. And Oel added some thanks for the things he had seen and learned that day. Grandfather smiled.

Dinner was eaten slowly that evening. Grandfather thought it was due to their fatigue, but Oel was trying to listen to the insects, birds, and other animals in the forest below them. He could hear the breeze brushing past his ears. It seemed chewing food made too much noise to hear those things. And he wanted to hear them. He was finding those sounds comforting. The sun had dropped below the horizon by the time Oel was finishing his last bite of food. The sky there was glowing gold, and then orange, and then red as the sun dipped. Soon, the grays of the evening encroached on the colors, and darkness came.

Oel asked, "Grandfather, can you tell me about each of the four dragons? What they were like? What they did after God sent them down to the earth? What are all the dragon signs that we didn't see today?"

Grandfather laid back, staring up into the sky as some stars began to appear and slowly became brighter as the darkness of night deepened. Then, he began to tell what legend said about dragons.

## CHAPTER 4

## THE RED DRAGON

The fires were raging and their filaments twisted and intertwined as they flowed back and forth in the ether of the heavens. The fiery fingers would weave themselves into glowing orbs and then stab out into the darkness around them. The orbs would expand and contract, pulsing with the terrible heat of the fire. Some would spread themselves across the heavens like a glowing veil. This was the fire from which the stars and sun were born. And this was the fire from which God took embers to create the red dragon. The embers grew into a pyre, and from the pyre formed the shape of the dragon. It was the dragon of fire. God named the dragon Pyrope.

Pyrope was the largest creature God had created up to that point. It was a marvelously grand creation! The beast had a long neck that allowed it to move its head in any direction, even over its back. Its head was long and bony, with ridges around its glowing red eyes that some people called "fiery-eyed" because it seemed the flames of fire were in them. Its snout was ribbed and had two nostrils at its tip from which vapors of smoke would roll forth. The dragon's mouth was long and full of dagger-like teeth, and its tongue was snake-like and forked at its tip. The dragon could swell its throat and spit spears of fire from its mouth. Down the dragon's back were broad spikes that looked like shields and ran from the back of its neck to the tip of its tail. Its body was broad and muscular, as was its long tail. At the tip of the tail were four short spikes that were sharp enough to pierce anything.

The dragon had four legs, two short ones and two longer ones. The short legs were more like arms and hands, and the longer ones were thick and powerful. At the end of each foot or hand were sharp claws that could tear apart the strongest iron. From each of its sides the dragon had long and powerful wings. Its wings could easily lift the beast so it could fly quickly and quietly, or they could wrap around its body like a blanket. Pyrope's entire body was covered with thick scales that overlapped in a way such that almost nothing could get between them and poke into its flesh. The scales were red from the fires that made the dragon, but sometimes could look black if the angle of light striking them was just right.

Pyrope made its home, its den, in the furnaces of the earth where the internal fires blazed constantly. Some people called such places volcanoes. But Pyrope also made its home in mountains that did not blaze. Few people knew exactly where Pyrope had its den, but many had seen the dragon flying overhead. The dragon's flights usually occurred at night when it was difficult to see it. It was indeed the rare occasion when the dragon was spotted flying during the day. Typically, Pyrope flew high in the sky and in large circular paths. That made it possible for the dragon to search for things harmful to God's creation and then swiftly dive down in a fiery trail to strike and eliminate them.

Despite Pyrope's frightening appearance, God had given the dragon a good heart and high intelligence. He created Pyrope to be a powerful creature that could quickly and easily complete tasks God gave it to do. In the beginning, Pyrope was a good and kind beast. But that changed as time went on. Lucifer had touched Pyrope's heart and planted a spot of dark evil there that would slowly grow until it eventually took over the dragon's entire heart. As that darkness grew, Pyrope became more and more fearsome and cruel. The dragon had learned to use its strengths for destructive purposes, and had learned it could garner for itself whatever it wanted. Pyrope became known to be greedy and malevolent. It gathered for itself vast treasure that it guarded jealously.

At first, Pyrope did what God wanted and performed acts of goodness. The dragon protected much of what God had created, and did it well. But then along came people who had chosen to not believe in God or follow His teachings closely. Those people were weak in faith.

Like Pyrope in its later years, they were often greedy. They would lie and steal and plot to take from others what they did not earn or deserve. And it was those people Lucifer used to turn Pyrope's heart darker and darker.

To begin, Lucifer planted the idea in their minds that Pyrope had a hoard of treasure that they could take. It made sense to them because they had seen the dragon flying overhead all throughout the country, and thought the dragon's den was somewhere in the mountains nearby. So those people set out to find the den and rob Pyrope of the treasure. Over the years, there were many expeditions up into the mountains to find Pyrope's den, but neither the den nor the treasure were ever found. However, in their search, the people laid ruin to many places in the mountains through their digging and scrounging. That damage to the land hurt Pyrope, and the dragon began to increasingly resent the people being up in the mountains. To take revenge, Pyrope began taking any treasure the people might have. The dragon was very efficient and effective in collecting gold, silver, copper, jewels, and anything else considered valuable. The dragon dens were becoming stuffed full of treasure. Anyone who dared get too near those dens quickly found themselves in peril and under the death sentence of the dragon. Pyrope jealously guarded every coin, every little piece, every glistening gem. Hence, no treasure hunter survived. So, the dark spot on Pyrope's heart grew darker and larger.

Later, Lucifer planted the idea in people's minds that Pyrope was a danger to them, and the best way to rid themselves of that danger was to slay Pyrope. As a result, the kings and rulers would send forth knights to find and kill the dragon. They were called dragon slayers. This went on for hundreds of years, and each time Pyrope would suffer injuries caused by the knights' weapons. Their special swords might slice into the dragon's foot. Their spears and lances sometimes pierced the dragon's sides. Most knights brought with them shields to protect them from Pyrope's fire, only to discover the metal would melt and be useless as any protection. Some knights shot arrows into Pyrope's neck, but that only made the dragon angrier. Each of the knights perished in their quest, and that infuriated the kings and rulers who responded by sending even more dragon slayers to find Pyrope. Some kings sent armies to slay the dragon, but they were no match for a giant flying dragon whose fiery breath scorched them and whose tail swept them aside and over the edges of the mountains. Pyrope's roar was so tremendous it sometimes shattered the armor knights wore. All this caused Pyrope to resent the people even more, and the dark spot on the dragon's heart grew.

At one point in time, Pyrope thought that if an important person could be held as prisoner in the dragon den, then the people would cease their attacks. Sometimes, the kings would offer their daughters, the princesses, to the dragon in an effort of appeasement. When princesses were not available, the people chose young maidens to be offered. Once Pyrope accepted those offers, the attacks seemed to become less frequent. Yet it was inevitable that there would be someone, usually a knight or prince, who decided to find Pyrope and rescue the princesses and maidens. Their efforts were harsh and caused the dragon much distress. By then, Pyrope's heart had hardened and was darker than night. The dragon reasoned the only way to stop the rescue efforts was to kill the young women, which it did. That, in turn, angered the people more, and they increased their attacks on the dragon.

After uncountable injuries and not being able to live peacefully, anger so filled the dragon that it took flight and soared above the people's towns to then swoop down and belch fire upon them. Pyrope burned to the ground many towns and many castles. The dragon's tail swept people aside, flinging them high into the air and over cliffs. The dragon's legs rammed walls and towers and ramparts and smashed them into rubble. This instilled more fear and hatred in the hearts of the people, who increased their efforts to slay the dragon. Finally, Pyrope decided to eliminate all those people once and for all, and attacked the mountain on which they had built all their castles and villages. The dragon braced itself and flew to the mountain, and once there circled the mountain many times. Each time Pyrope circled the mountain, it spewed scorching fire down onto the mountain and burned everything and everyone in sight. Pyrope was so thorough that the entire mountain was left charred and blackened. The blackening was so intense that nothing ever again grew on that mountain. Even centuries later, the mountain remains charred. No one goes to that mountain any more. It is known as Pyrope Peak.

## CHAPTER 5

## THE BLUE DRAGON

The lower waters churned and bubbled as they swept across the face of the earth and filled the lowlands and basins. The upper waters swirled and lashed across the skies, driving itself down to the ground as torrents of rain. Streams and rivers formed through which the waters tumbled and rushed on their way to what would become the seas. Their roaring turbulence was violent, cutting their way through soil and rock and carrying along debris ripped from the earth. Water spray filled the air across the lands. As the waters slowed, some settled into places that became ponds and lakes. Some slowed and stayed within the riverbanks and streambeds, and some added to the volume of the seas. Once the waters had settled and become mostly still, God collected a drop from each place where water existed. He took a drop from each sea, from each lake and each pond, from each river and stream, and from the spray in the air. There were so many places of water that God's collection was an immeasurable volume. The collected drops swirled and mixed and drew together, clinging together one to the next. The collection's surface rippled and bubbled and shifted one way and then the other. It was the deepest blue in color, and only the kind of blue God could create.

It was bluer than the sky. God held the collection of drops between His hands, pressing it together, and it began to take the shape of a dragon. It was the dragon of water. God named the dragon Nilakanta.

Nilakanta was a long and slender dragon. Its head was similar to Pyropes, but more slender and streamlined, almost having the shape of a horses' head. It had a short horn protruding from its forehead just above its two deep blue eyes that glistened and contained swirls like those made from torrents of water. There were large frills surrounding the dragon's ears, and the frills would expand and widen or contract and narrow, depending upon the dragon's mood. Nilakanta's snout was pointed, and its nostrils would open wide or close tightly as it breathed water. The dragon's mouth was filled with long sword-like teeth that would criss-cross whenever the mouth was closed. Nilakanta's neck was only half as long as Prypoe's, but it was still long enough to enable the dragon to turn its head and see all around it, over its back, and under its belly. The dragon's tail was as long as its neck and had two horizontal fins protruding from either side of its tip. All along the dragon's back, from the base of it neck to near the tip of its tail, were raised ridges or humps. The largest were at the middle of the dragon's back and the sizes became smaller as they progressed either toward the neck or toward the tail.

Nilakanta had four legs, and each ended with a broad foot. From the front of each foot extended sharp claws, and between the claws was webbing that allowed Nilakanta to swim quickly through any water. Nilakanta had two wings, one attached to the middle of its left side and one to its right. The entire surface of the dragon was covered with small scales that were colored with a mix of different blues and greens, giving the dragon a shimmering appearance like water-soaked leather.

In the beginning, Nilakanta was known for its wisdom and valor, and some people found good fortune whenever the dragon was nearby. That did not necessarily mean they became rich or wealthy. More often, it meant they would have a plentiful harvest of fish or be safe in their journeys across the waters. The dragon resided in the bottoms of the seas or sometimes at the bottoms of lakes. At times, it would cruise along just under the surface of water, causing wakes to form behind it. In some unknown way, it could move from one body of water to another without being seen.

Nilakanta knew the dangers that would come if people did harm to the seas and lakes, and would try to guide them to live more in harmony with what the earth could provide. But as the number of people increased, they ignored Nilakanta's warnings and began to overfish the waters. They began to dig and destroy shorelines as they built cities and castles too close to the water. As those things happened, misfortune started to plague the people. The number of fish they could harvest started to decrease, and hunger started to become common. Waves from the waters would erode the shoreline and undercut building foundations and wharves and docks, causing them to crumble and fall into the seas. It was becoming more frequent that people would become ill from drinking water near the places where their wastes were finding the way into the rivers, lakes, and seas.

It was then when Lucifer planted an idea in the minds of the people. The idea was that their misfortunes were being caused by Nilakanta. It was the idea that Nilakanta was acting against the best interests of the people, and was punishing them for trying to get and do things they believed necessary for living life as they wanted. In their stubbornness and anger, the people failed to see the wrongs they were committing, and instead concluded the answer to their ills was to rid themselves of Nilakanta. So, they built higher and bigger wave breaker walls along their shorelines. They more than doubled the number of ships in their fleet, and armed the ships with harpoons, cannon, and other weapons intended to harm or kill Nilakanta. Flotillas were sent to sea with the sole purpose of hunting down the dragon.

During the early encounters, Nilakanta simply tried to

outmaneuver the people's ships. But as their ships became larger and faster, the dragon's attempts became less successful. Then, the dragon tried to manipulate the people by causing them to hallucinate and see things in the waters that were not there and to not see things that were there. The dragon gave them hallucinations of huge boulders sticking up out of the water, or of reefs and shallow shoals. They were given hallucinations of not seeing the schools of fish they sought during their fishing expeditions. Even still, the people continued to hunt Nilakanta. This caused the dark spot on the dragon's heart to grow and become darker. And the dragon started thinking about harming the people.

Nilakanta's attacks on people began as their hunting ships drew near. The dragon would give a huge flap of its wings, creating giant waves that washed over the ships and made them sink. Sometimes, the dragon would whip its tail and smash the wooden ships into small pieces. Despite that, some of the sailors were able to strike Nilananta with their harpoons or shots from their guns. Each time the dragon was hit and injured, the dark spot on its heart grew and became darker. As time went on, Nilakanta's attacks on ships became more and more indiscriminate. Whether or not a ship was a fishing ship, a hunting warship, or simply a transport ship, the dragon would do what it could to sink it. Many people lost their lives at sea because of that. In response, the people made even more ships and equipped them with more powerful weapons.

Nilakanta started to reason that perhaps the best way to stop the hunting would be to prevent the people from setting sail from their docks in the first place. So, the dragon whipped up violent storm after violent storm. The storms would batter any ships out on the water and throw them upon rocky shores and reefs. They would wash out to sea docks and houses built along shorelines. The dragon generated so many storms that people started calling their times the "age of storms." People became more fearful of setting sail on the waters or living near the shores, but there was a hardened core of them who became even more determined to rid themselves of Nilakanta. This, in turn, caused the dark spot on the dragon's heart to grow even more and darker still.

The dragon then decided to put an end to the people. Nilakanta spent a few weeks at the bottom of the sea gathering its strength and powers. At the end, the dragon arose from the depths and with the mightiest of roars stirred up the sea and the winds and the storms. The dragon swam toward the coastline cities and once near them opened its mouth wide to breathe water on them. From its mouth shot out gigantic streams of water with hurricane force, causing all the stone water breakers to crumble and all the houses to collapse. Then the dragon's waves grew and grew until they were the size of small mountains. The waves raced toward the shore and smashed into it with such force nothing could withstand it. Everything along the shoreline and up the sides of the mountains was submerged under water, and when the waters withdrew back to the lakes and seas, all evidence of people had been washed away. Some of the lakes were now connected to the seas and the seas to the lakes. Slowly, the waters receded and settled in the low spaces. Aside from the sea, the largest basin of water is what has become known as Nilakanta Lake.

## CHAPTER 6

## THE BROWN DRAGON

The solid earth formed in fits of rumbling and rolling. It was to have a firmness, yet it would still shift and shudder as the raw material that formed it settled into its place. The center became a core that remained hot and molten as the substances that made up the rest of the earth encircled it and insulated it from the outside. Above the molten mass was hot stone that squeezed and oozed its way along paths it took as it flowed around the broiling core. It flowed slowly and with difficulty, some of it pushing up and some down, some bunching and some stretching, causing it to have folds of rises and dips all along its surface.

The rest of what made the earth came to rest on top of the undulating ooze as if it was particles of dust or sand settling onto the ground after a desert wind storm. More and more of it settled until it made a thick layer enveloping the whole globe. Some settled more easily and more quickly than the rest. The heavier and larger parts sank their way to the lower levels of the earth while the lighter and smaller parts drifted down like a blanket that coated the lower ones. Within this were formed rocks and stones and soils of all kinds. The oozing part would shift and push and pull and warp the outer layer of the earth, causing it to wrinkle and shake or stretch and sag. From those movements arose the great mountains, the deep valleys of the earth, and the broad plains that stretched to the horizon.

It was upon those places that God enrooted the plants to cover the earth with their greenness. But not everywhere was blessed with plants. There remained places that were barren and dry. After the earth had formed, God began scooping small parts of it into His hands. Some parts He took from the fertile soils of the expansive plains. Some parts He took from the barren deserts. Other parts He took from the lush valleys, and still other parts from the hard and craggy mountains. He scooped mud and rock and stone and all manner of earth substances. There was no part of the earth from which God did not scoop something. Then, God cupped His hands together and squeezed everything tightly, causing it to begin taking on another form. Once God opened His hands, what rested there was a dragon. It was the dragon of the earth. God named it Petrous.

Petrous was a large dragon, but looked squat and compact. It gave off a sense of being muscularly dense. The dragon's head was broad and flat, resembling the shape of a giant salamander. It had no frills or horns on its head, but where its forehead should be was a large, flat, thick shield of bone. The bone shield extended out just a little beyond the sides of the rest of the head as if making a covering for the dragon's eyes. The dragon's eyes were a dark brown with a grainy-earthy texture. Its eyes were surrounded by thick flaps of skin above and below that could act as eyelids and close to cover the eyes completely. Petrous' snout was short and rounded and had a bony plate covering its tip. Petrous' mouth was very wide, and from it could extend a thick rounded tongue.

From all appearances, the dragon had almost no neck. What neck it had was very thick and strong, but limited the dragon's head movements so it could not turn just its head to see behind itself. The dragon's body had a flat profile to it. Its back was almost flat and was shaped like an stretched-out shield. That shape revealed a thick bony plate covering the entire back of the dragon. Down the middle of the back shield ran a ridge of short spikes, and similar spikes protruded from the edges of the shield all along the dragon's sides. Its tail was not long and ended with two large spikes at its tip. Unlike the other dragons, Petrous had no wings. Petrous had four legs, and each was short but exceptionally stout. At the end of each leg was a broad and thick foot. Short thick claws extended from each toe. The dragon's body was covered from the tip of its nose to the tip of its tail with overlapping brown scales that looked more like flat stones than scales.

Petrous was made to easily burrow its way through rock and soil and do so quickly. As it made its way through the earth, it would pull stones, rocks, soil, and just about anything else into its mouth and consume it. If there was more than Petrous needed or wanted, it would eject it with tremendous force from its mouth.

Petrous had dug many tunnels and burrows through the mountains as it moved about, and carved out many caves as well. Petrous was an earth-breathing dragon and had a keen knowledge of where valuable resources were hiding beneath the earth's surface. However, the dragon's primary interest was providing ways for animals to move safely through the mountains, for fresh air to pass from one side of the mountain to another, and keep the mountains and lands healthy.

People living on the mountains where Petrous lived benefitted from the tunnels and burrows the dragon created over many years. Although Petrous had little interest in the precious metals and gemstones located within the depths of the earth, the people did. The tunnels and burrows made it easy for them to journey into the earth to find and retrieve gold, silver, copper, and gemstones. The profits they made from that bounty enabled them to live splendidly.

It seemed the people had everything they could want. But what seemed to be was not what was reality to them.

The more valuables the people removed from the earth, the more they seemed to want. The more their lifestyles improved, the more lavish they wanted it to be. There was no end to what they wanted. Their greed drove them to go into the tunnels and burrows and scratch out even the smallest pieces of metal or gems. Some people would become territorial and protective of certain places and not allow others to search or mine in those places. In a brief amount of time, people began fighting with each other over who owned a tunnel or who could have access to it.

The situation became more serious when there were no more precious metals or gemstones to be found in the existing tunnels and burrows. They began harming one another. Their leaders called everyone together to talk about the problem. It was then when Lucifer planted dark ideas in their minds. Instead of thinking of ways to live within their means and share with each other, the ideas were about who to blame for their shortage of the wealth they craved. And the ideas were that all these problems were ultimately the fault of Petrous. It was Petrous who had failed to dig enough tunnels, to make enough burrows, to excavate enough caves. It was the dragon's fault for failing to expose valuable veins of precious metals or deposits of gemstones. The idea was that Petrous was now keeping those things for itself, and that angered the people.

At first, the people were certain there must be more valuables not far from where most of them had been collected in the past. Some were sure there was more to be had hiding just behind the walls of the tunnels, burrows, and caves. So, in their way of thinking, they just needed to expand the walls of those places or dig their own tunnels nearby.

Many mining projects were started, and many problems arose because of them. As tunnel walls were expanded, their walls and ceilings became weaker and less stable. That resulted in cave-ins, trapping and injuring many miners. Similar results occurred when digging was done in caves. Further, all the extra digging produced waste rock and stone that had to be taken from the tunnels and caves and thrown off to the sides near their entrances. Those piles of discarded rock and stone were unstable and sometimes collapsed, rushing down the mountainsides and causing damage to houses and buildings below the mines. Water from rain or from streams running down the mountains would seep through the piles and exit them filled with poisonous materials that had been clinging to the stones. Living conditions for the people steadily became worse and worse along with the decrease in wealth. There were increased health problems, and people were more tired and sore from having to do so much work for so little gain. All of this, in their thinking of course, was the fault of Petrous.

Eventually, some of the people decided the answer to their troubles was to capture Petrous and force the dragon to do the digging for them. They convinced everyone else to agree to the same solution. All the people then turned their attentions and energies to tracking down Petrous. Nothing else mattered to them. Different groups selected different tunnels, burrows, or caves to go into. They armed themselves with nets, ropes, chains, and anything else they thought might be helpful for trapping and holding the dragon. They took with them picks and shovels, chisels and hammers, and other tools to dig traps for Petrous.

All that below-ground activity disturbed Petrous, making the dragon move from one place to another in an effort to put some distance between it and the people. Yet the disturbances kept coming, and Petrous began to resent what the people were doing. The dark spot on the dragon's heart grew, and it became darker.

More and more people joined the search for Petrous, and with that came more and more disturbance and digging. Once in a while, a group would catch sight of the dragon and try to capture it. Petrous would escape their tries and withdraw deeper into the mountains. And the dark spot on its heart grew further. The dragon's escapes angered the people more, and their anger turned to wanting revenge. They wanted to kill Petrous for what it had done to them, and their nets and ropes and chains were replaced with weapons. In the few times they managed to draw near the dragon, their weapons injured it and the dragon's anger against the people increased. The dark spot on Petrous' heart grew even more.

The assaults on Petrous continued and increased in intensity until the dragon finally decided it had to be stopped. So, the dragon clawed into the earth, made new burrows, and created landslides that sent rocks and stones crashing down upon villages and towns. Landslides also covered the entrances to many of the tunnels and burrows trapping people inside who were unfortunate enough to be inside them. When the people brought in machines to remove the rubble and resume their searching attacks on Petrous, the dragon dove deeper into the earth and with its claws caused earthquakes that shook everything to its roots. Yet the people persisted in their goal to kill Petrous. And the dark spot on the dragon's heart grew yet again, and became much darker.

Finally, the dragon had enough, and decided to put an end to it. When the people were all resting in their homes before another attack, Petrous quickly burrowed toward their villages. As soon as the dragon broke through the surface of the earth, it forcibly breathed out streams of rocks and stones with such strength and speed that it piled up as walls that wrapped around entire mountains. The walls were so thick and tall that nobody could get past them. There were no openings or gates in those walls through which anyone could escape. There was not enough time for anyone to dig beneath them. Petrous made multiple walls at different heights up the mountain sides so people from one part of the mountain could not go to the rescue of others. Once the walls of stone were in place, the dragon created earthquakes and landslides that buried everything between each of the walls. At the end, there was no sign of any human habitation. No buildings or houses or other structures were visible. There was not a single person remaining who had not been buried. All of them were now gone. And the mountains were quiet. No one dares go to those places. The closest mountain where the dragon's wrath can be seen is known as Petrous Point.

## CHAPTER 7

## THE WHITE DRAGON

Above the solid earth and the seas, but below the heavens and the sun and stars, the air of the world was formed. Unlike the waters or soils or rocks, unlike the fires of the inner earth or volcanos, the air was not something that could be touched. It was not something that could be seen. Instead, it was something that could be felt. The presence of air could only be known by feeling or seeing the way it influenced and effected other things of the earth.

As the air rested above the surface of the earth, it itself was not seen, but the winds within it could rustle the leaves and branches of trees so the effects of the air would be visible. The winds could be great or they could be small. They could be soothing, calm, and constructive; or they could be violent, churning, and destructive. The air would release moisture to form visible clouds that would form, grow, and billow, and it would gather moisture causing the clouds to melt and fade away. Some clouds would drift lazily across the sky, while some would become dark and stormy and violent. Some clouds crept next to the ground, while some reached so high they were made of ice.

The winds in the air would move the clouds across

the face of the earth, up over the mountains, down through the valleys, and across the great expanses of seas and plains. Invisible gyres and turbulence could churn the air, generating either great torrential storms or unusual calmness.

The air had no smell to it, but it would hold the odors from things that offered them such as the sweetness of flowers or the pungence of smoke. The air was made to envelop the entire earth, and it allowed animals and plants to breathe.

Once the air was made, God began to gather parts of it together. He gathered air from the peaks of mountains, from the depths of valleys, and from above the desert sands and above the seas. He gathered air from high in the sky where it almost touched the stars and where it hugged near to the ground. He gathered air from the north, from the south, from the east, and from the west. With the air, God gathered glistening crystals of ice floating in the air above glaciers or in wispy horsetail clouds from the highest parts of the sky. He gathered the odors and smells carried in the air, and even the winds that made the air their home. He gathered different parts of different clouds, as well as the colors the air could make as the sun's rays pierced it at different times of the day. Once God had gathered that air, He took a deep breath and inhaled it all. Then He cupped His hands and blew gently into them. As His breath settled into His hands, it took the shape of a dragon. It was the dragon of the air. God named the dragon Brenna.

Brenna was a slender dragon, but it was large. The dragon's head was long and slender and shaped much like that of a crocodile. There were rows of low ridges running across the tip of the nose and up across the forehead. A frill arose just where the head met the neck, and it could fold flat or be raised like a sail. The dragon's mouth was narrow and contained glistening white teeth that were sharp like the tips of the shaprest of spears. The dragon's tongue was long and narrow, and widened at its tip into a flat spoon-shape. Brenna's neck was long and slender, and allowed the dragon to move its head in virtually any direction, including backward over its back.

Down the length of the Brenna's back were three ridges. The main ridge extended from the top of the dragon's neck to the tip of its tail. Two other ridges ran parallel to the main ridge, just slightly lower on the dragon's sides than the main ridge, but started at the base of the neck and ended at the base of the tail. All three ridges did not appear to be very tall, but could expand and extend outward like long sails. Brenna's body shape was something like that of an eagle. At times, especially during flight, that shape could become more flattened to enhance the dragon's ability to glide and fly.

The dragon had four legs, the front two being small compared to the back two. Each of the legs was slender and not overly muscular. Adorning each front leg was a hand-like foot with short claws on each toe. Each back leg had a long three-toed foot, with each toe having a long sharp talon. Along the length of each leg was a fin that extended from near the ankle up to the top of the thigh. The fins were useful in helping the dragon steer through the air during flight.

Brenna's tail was long and streamlined, and ended with a dolphin-like fin at its tip. The dragon had two wings protruding from each of its sides. The front wings were small and could be tucked in close to the body. The large back wings were just in front of the dragon's back hips and looked like eagle wings except there were no feathers. The coverings of the wings and body were overlapping teardrop-shaped scales where the larger ends faced the front. Each scale was opalescent white, and glimmered in sunlight. If seen from a certain angle, the scales made the dragon look like clear glass crystal. At other angles, the dragon might look gold or silver.

When in flight, the dragon looked like blazing light that could blind anyone who looked directly at it. The dragon's coloring was such that when flying high in the sky it was virtually invisible, and it blended in especially well with the clouds. This referred to Brenna's name, which meant "out of the clouds in the sky." Brenna's skin beneath the scales was almost transparent, and if one looked closely at the dragon's chest the dragon's red heart could be seen beating.

Brenna's chest could expand to be about twice the size it normally was, and that enabled the dragon to breathe in vast amounts of air and then exhale it in jet-like streams with such force that it could topple buildings, flatten trees in forests, and shake mountains. The dragon could use its air breathing to create clouds or make them grow. Sometimes, the dragon could breathe out air to make huge storm clouds from which powerful winds and booming thunder would roll, strong enough to split houses in two.

God created Brenna for two purposes. The first was to bring bright light to the surface of the earth wherever darkness existed, and shine that light so intensely anything hidden in the dark would be revealed and driven away. The second was to draw from the purity of the air and use its power in tremendous jet-streaming gusts to blast away any darkness clinging to the earth. So, the dragon would take flight and sail through the upper regions of the sky searching for signs of darkness needing to be dispelled. Nobody really knew where Brenna nested when not flying, but legend spoke of the dragon coming to rest at the top of a high mountain palisade amongst a line of steep cliffs that overlooked everything below it.

The nature of people was twofold. First, there was goodness of heart. Second, there was evil of heart. For some people, the second nature grew and became dominant. The people chose to live lives of selfishness, depravity, greed, envy, misdeeds, lying, and other sinful things. They were often self-centered and took pleasure in harming others in order to gain things for themselves. These were people over whom Lucifer had much control. Some did not recognize the source of their sinfulness, while others did and welcomed it. Some sought to hide their deeds in the cloak of darkness and shadows, and pretended they were doing good works while doing just the opposite.

Having their actions brought to light was perhaps the biggest threat those people could imagine. And Brenna's purposes made the dragon a significant threat to their way of life. That made Brenna their enemy, and they actively sought ways to deceive the dragon and hide from it. Lucifer aided them in their deceptions. At first, they would do their activities and store their riches in houses that looked like those of good-natured people. But eventually, the dragon would discover what was happening, and would generate towering storm clouds releasing horrendous thunder that caused those houses to shudder and shatter. That angered the people, and they sought other ways to deceive the dragon. The dragon was fulfilling the purpose for which it was created, and the dark spot on its heart failed to grow.

Then, those people attempted to do their deeds in the depths of the thick forests. The tree canopies provided excellent camouflage and shielded activities on the ground from overhead view. They misused the goodness of the natural world to do unnatural things. Yet Brenna still found ways to detect them, and reduced their perversions to splinters. That angered the evil-natured people who then vowed to defeat the dragon. And all along, the dark spot on the dragon's heart failed to grow.

Next, Lucifer encouraged the evil-natured people to construct hidden places where they could stash their ill-gotten gains and then use them to buy weapons for attacking the dragon. They dug basements, dungeons, and tunnels in which they would conduct their dark business. They bought and stockpiled their weapons. When Brenna discovered those places, it would use its powerful air-breathing to quake and shatter the ground and bury the hiding places so they would be of no use to anyone and nothing could be retrieved from them. The evil-natured people were angered and frustrated each time this happened. And each time, the dark spot on the dragon's heart remained the same: small and ungrowing.

Lucifer prodded those people further and planted into their minds ideas about increasing their cruelty against others, reaping from them valuables that would be used to fund their attacks on the dragon. So, they gathered into mobs to attack the treasuries of good cities and plunder them. They sought gold and other precious metals. They sought sparkling gems, rare spices, and other goods. They planned to abuse villagers and burn their homes, and planned to enslave them and sell them for profit. Some were going to kill villagers for the pleasure of doing it. This was, of course, some of the darkest activity a people could do. Such darkness would certainly fail to be hidden from Brenna. So, the dragon flew to the dark village and swept down upon them, flinging its tail from side to side sweeping away many of those with evil in their hearts. Then the dragon rose into the air and inhaled so much air that its chest doubled in size, and with an ear-splitting roar unleashed that air into the mobs knocking them asunder. The evil mobs were completely defeated, and had no choice but to withdraw. That angered the evil-natured people to the point of delirium. And still the dark spot on the dragon's heart could not grow.

In their delirium, Lucifer held great sway over those people and emboldened them to seek out Brenna's mountain palisade and kill the dragon. And after killing the dragon, they would turn their armies on the rest of the world to conquer them. They sent word out throughout the land for like-minded people to gather as armies and bring with them all the weapons they could carry. They gathered their wagons, oxen, and tents, and their armies joined together. Then, they set off to find the palisade. Scouts were sent forward to find the dragon's home, and pioneers were positioned in the lead to make roads for the army to follow.

After years of searching, the scouts finally declared they had located the palisades. The various armies concentrated their forces before the palisades and advanced their attack. As the armies made their way up the mountainside, Brenna arose from the palisade, lifted itself to the highest parts of the sky, and with the rush of air around it swooped down with the sound of roaring thunder that shattered the people's hearing. The dragon spread its four wings and directed the bedazzling rays of the sun with such brilliance that it blinded the attackers and they could no longer find their way. Then, Brenna hovered above them, inhaled as much pure air as its chest could hold, and expelled it with such force that each person of the armies was crushed and driven into the ground. No one dares go to that place anymore, and it is known as Brenna Palisade. And the dark spot on the dragon's heart remained small.

## CHAPTER 8

## STREAMS OF LIFE

By the time Grandfather had completed telling Oel about the legends of each of the four dragons, the first tips of morning sunbeams were beginning to light up the eastern sky. An orange-gold halo glowed at the point where the sun would be climbing up over the distant mountains. A few low-lying clouds had grey linings on their tops but were starting to look like orange and red fire on their bottoms. The storytelling had taken the entire night. Yet neither Oel nor Grandfather seemed tired. There was something invigorating about the legends. Both stood up, inhaled deeply, and sighed with a big stretch of their backs and arms.

Without speaking, each stooped down and began rolling his blanket and fastening with its rope ties. Oel put his blanket roll on the ground and sat on it. Grandfather looked at him, smiled, and agreed that was a good idea. Then, they said a morning prayer, and afterward opened their satchels to remove food for their breakfast. There was not much food left in the satchels. It would be a lean breakfast. That also meant there would be nothing for lunch. Oel wondered if Grandfather had failed to plan enough for their food needs. But that didn't match what Oel knew about Grandfathers' meticulous and careful planning habits. He always seemed to plan down to the smallest details and do so thoroughly.

Oel asked, "Grandfather, our food will be gone after breakfast. What are we going to do for the rest of the day's food?"

Grandfather smiled. "The land will provide it for us. We won't go hungry. In fact, we will probably have more than we need."

Oel thought that with their satchels now empty, there would not be as much weight to manage as they made their way back down the mountain toward home. That would be a blessing. The upward climbs and walking of the past two days were starting to show their toll on them. Fatigue was tugging at them from every direction, and it would be easy to just sit for the entire day and rest. But there was more to do, and a good distance to go before the day was done.

When the two had everything packed, Oel started walking toward the path they had used when coming up two days before. Grandfather reached out and put his hand on Oel's shoulder and stopped him.

"Not that way today." said Grandfather. "We have another way to go."

Grandfather turned Oel part way around and motioned that they would be leaving the rock ledge from its far end. Oel thought that would be taking them further from the way home, but trusted Grandfather knew best about what would be necessary for the day's journey.

The new pathway was every bit as rough as the old one. There were places where it was steep and strewn with boulders, and other places where it was more level and covered with loose fragments of stone and pebbles. Oel and Grandfather skillfully used their walking sticks to help them move aside around loose rocks. The new day's sunlight gave the brown rocks an almost golden hue and the shadows from the trees helped hold in the chill of the night air. Grandfather led the way, and Oel thought he was moving much too fast at times. Oel would have liked to take it more slowly. That good old fatigue was speaking to him. But the two pressed on down the mountainside.

About half way through the morning, Oel began to hear a different sound coming from amongst the trees in front of them. At first, it was faint, but the further they walked the louder the sound became. It started like a distant rumble, and grew into a quiet roaring. Oel saw Grandfather stop between two trees and stand still. When Oel caught up to him, he stood still, too. Before them was a waterfall. The water was racing over the rocks and tumbling down with a loudness that made Oel want to cover his ears. It looked like the water was boiling as it churned and twisted down the rocks. Mist rose up from the bottom of the waterfall so thick at times it obscured the view of the other side of the stream. At the bottom of the waterfall and just a little further downstream was a jumble of rocks and boulders. The rushing water fought its way over them making white foam and swirling eddies. Oel and Grandfather stood a while admiring the grandeur of the water spectacle. It was almost breathtaking! Soon, Grandfather motioned with his arm to indicate they needed to walk further down the bank of the stream.

Once Oel and Grandfather were downstream enough to be able speak and hear each other over the roaring waterfall, Grandfather told Oel they should sit for a minute or two. He pointed to a couple of rocks on the high riverbank where they quickly deposited themselves.

"Oel, I want you to look at the river and the valley around it. Tell me what you see." said Grandfather.

Oel looked around and replied, "Well, I see the rushing water. And the river seems to be running through the bottom of the valley between the two sides of the mountain. The riverbanks are very steep, and they are just rocks. It looks like the river has cut its way downward through the rocks."

Grandfather smiled, "Yes, the river has cut its way down through the rocks. And it has cut down deeply into them. That is why the river is at the bottom of a valley with very steep walls on either side of it. If you look further, you will see that the path the river is taking is almost straight. The fast waters keep its path that way. This part of the river is young. It is making itself. It is much like the life of people."

Oel frowned. "How is it like the life of people?" he asked.

Grandfather explained. "When people are young, it seems their lives are full of energy and force. They fling themselves headlong so quickly that they sometimes tumble over the edge and plunge into the unknown without really knowing where they are going. They rush forward through things, through life, cutting their way along whatever path they choose to take. They are seemingly unaware of many things around them and cut along straight to what they think they want. All the while, they run into obstacles, perhaps other people or situations, but they do not slow down. They hit them head-on and that causes turbulence, like the boulder rapids not far from the waterfall. Sometimes that turbulence causes swirling eddies as if the flow of life is confused about the ways it needs to go. It is during this time of life when one seems to set his course and establish the way he will go through life that is yet to come. For most, this is a time in life when changing the course, changing the direction, is difficult or impossible.

Later, one might realize that the boulders they've encountered were just trying to slow them down a little so they could rush less and think more deeply about where they are heading."

Oel slowly nodded his head in understanding. "Where am I in life's stream, Grandfather?"

"I think you have hit the boulders and started to slow a bit. You are coming to see those boulders not as hindrances, but as something that is helping you understand more about what life should be about and how you should live it. But you still want to move fast!"

Oel giggled. "Yes, I like to move fast. I like to get from one place to the next as fast as I can. I don't like getting delayed in doing what I want or need to do."

"I know." said Grandfather. "But I think you are beginning to see there are times when you need to take things a little more slowly. You are beginning to see the importance of slowing down, stopping once in a while, and looking at life around you. It is like our trek up to the mountain summit. We could have rushed up there, eaten our lunch, and immediately started on our way back home. If we had done so, think about all the things you saw that you would have missed. Think about the things you've learned that you would not have learned. Some people, unfortunately, never find out about how important it is to slow down and let life speak to them."

Oel grinned. "Yes! I want life to speak to me! Let's go!" and he pointed along the downstream path as he giggled.

Grandfather laughed and pulled himself up off his rock seat.

As the two walked through the forest, Oel tried to take his steps just a little more slowly than normal. He would pause here and there to stare past the path and deep into the forest to see what might be visible, or to hear what the forest might be saying. He seemed to see more animal signs amongst the trees, as well as weather signs and the signs of the time of day. He seemed to hear the trees, the shrubs, the scittering and calls of the animals that he normally would not have paid attention to or heard before. He was finding himself immersed in the richness of the life of the forest, and not just walking through clusters of trees.

The denseness of the forest was increasing. The trees seemed taller and closer together. Oel could feel how the trees were cooling the air with the light breeze meandering through them. He could see from the shadows and spaces between the limbs that it was nearly noon. His stomach started to rumble. Time for lunch! But they had eaten the remainder of their food up on the rock ledge high on the mountainside.

"Grandfather, I'm hungry." said Oel.

"Me, too!" said Grandfather. "Let's gather our lunch that nature is providing for us!"

Oel didn't know what Grandfather meant by "Let's gather our lunch!" So, he looked at Grandfather with a quizzical expression.

Grandfather said, "Come and watch closely." and stepped off the riverbank right into the stream. The water in the stream was flowing quickly and smoothly, but not roaring as it was back near the waterfall. It was clear and Oel could see the pebbles and rocks on the bottom of the stream. Grandfather walked out into the water slowly until he was in it up to his thighs. Then, he stood still, bending forward slowly, and extending his arms until his hands nearly touched the water.

Suddenly, Grandfather struck his hands downward like knives, splashing the water, and then stood up. In his grasp was a squiggling fish! Grandfather tossed the fish onto the river bank next to Oel. "Your turn, Oel!" he said. So, Oel stepped out into the water and took a few steps toward Grandfather. "Oh!" squealed Oel. "The water is cold!" He shivered, and stepped further into the stream as Grandfather waved him forward. Once beside Grandfather, he stooped over as Grandfather had done, and peered down into the icy clear water.

Around his legs Oel could see something moving. It was not water. And it was many things! What he saw were fish. He could clearly see their silvery and redish sides as they wriggled their way through the water. When one swam close to his legs, Oel stabbed at it with his hands, trying to grasp it as Grandfather had done. There was a big splash, and Oel's face was dripping with water and his chest was soaked. And there was nothing in his hands. Grandfather laughed and tilted his head to the side with a nod, silently telling Oel to try again.

Oel shook himself a little to rid himself of his newly acquired blanket of water, and positioned his body to try again. It took him several tries before he finally managed to grab one of the fish. He was so excited that he raised it above his head and began to dance. The next thing he heard was the hearty laughing of Grandfather. Oel's dancing feet had slipped out from under him and he went plunging backward down into the water! He spit water out of his mouth as he struggled to regain his stance, and then realized he had lost his prize fish. Water running off his head was blurring his vision, so he shook his head and wiped his face with his hands. He shivered, and without prodding from Grandfather regained his fishing stance. Moments later, he had another fish in his grasp.

Grandfather walked over to Oel and put his arm around his shoulder, and two made their way to the shore. Once there, they made a small fire and began cleaning the fish they had caught. Grandfather had Oel find two long sticks and sharpen the ends of them with a knife. Then they poked the sticks through the two fish and positioned the fish over the fire to cook them. As the fish were cooking, Grandfather took Oel into the forest to find some nuts and berries. They found some red elderberries, blackberries, persimmons, hickory nuts, and chestnuts and piled them into their upturned hats. It was not long before they returned to their camp with lunch in hand. The two said a prayer of thanksgiving for the bounty the land had yielded to them. Then it was time to munch and crunch through lunch. Oel thought this had to be the most satisfying lunch he had ever eaten.

As they two were finishing their lunch, Grandfather pointed to the river and asked Oel to take a close look at it and the valley around it. "Tell me what you see about the river, Oel." he said.

Oel looked carefully. "First, I see a lot of very cold running water!" He laughed. "But I also see the valley is not as deep as it was by the waterfall. The walls of the valley are not as steep as they were upstream. And the path the river is taking is not as straight. It has some curves in it."

"Good!" said Grandfather. "And that is also a lot like the lives of people."

Oel settled himself to hear more from Grandfather.

"You see," said Grandfather, "as people grow from

their childhood into being young adults, the flow of their lives changes. They are not usually as prone to rush wildly headlong as they did earlier in life. They are more controlled about things. They still have life that moves quickly, but it is with much less turbulence. As they go along in life's stream, they find they have to move a little from their original path to get through things. They may need to shift a little one way, and then the other way. That enables them to make the adjustments they need in order to get along in life.

If you look closely at places where the stream turns in its course, you will see some interesting things. At the inside of the curves, you'll see there are flat areas where sand and small pebbles have come to rest. At the outside of the curves, you will see the waters are cutting away at the riverbank and moving soil and rocks away. That is how it is in people's lives. As they make adjustments in their life paths, there are some things that get deposited and come to rest. Those are the responsibilities they've taken on, and the things they have accumulated . . . like homes and families and friends. Most of the time, those are calm places in life. They are gentle and quiet places to be. But some of those life adjustments bring with them the need to cut into new places. It sometimes means cutting away those things that might impair where one needs to go. That also introduces new things into the stream of life, and people need to be able to carry it along.  There are times when people must make drastic changes in the course of their lives, but many times those changes are relatively small.  But the changes all occur to achieve one thing.  That is to get one from a beginning to an end.  No matter what changes come or need to be made, the life waters still flow from their beginning toward their end.  None of its stops just because there is a bend in the stream.  Your parents are living their lives much like this part of the river."

Oel looked at the river more intensely. "I see those things in it, Grandfather. I see the river signs! I wonder, Grandfather, if the blue dragon has anything to do with how the waters flow? Is there dragon sign in the river?"

Grandfather gave a shrug. "Perhaps. But it isn't like the way the legend spoke about. There is something different about it. We'll speak more about that later. For now, it is time for us to move along."

By now, the forest seemed alive with birdsong and the rustling of brush as deer and other animals hurried here and there. Once in a while, one seemed brave enough to stand still and watch Oel and Grandfather on their walk. The leaves in the trees were almost singing as the breeze had grown into a soft wind. Their shaking and moving caused the sunbeams that penetrated down to the forest floor to dance first one way and then another. Oel felt as if he was seeing the life of the forest clearly for the first time. It seemed as if it had finally seeped down into the marrow of his bones.

It was about mid-afternoon when Oel and Grandfather came to an opening in the forest canopy. It wasn't a meadow. It was a place where a violent wind storm had once blasted its way through the trees. Oel could see many trees that had been broken, and some had been toppled and were lying on the ground. It was obvious the storm had come quite some time ago because the trees still standing had leaves on their branches and the grasses had grown up and around the fallen trunks of trees lying on the forest floor. As Oel and Grandfather meandered their way through the fallen timbers, they stopped to sit on one. Oel quickly realized that where they stopped was not by chance. Grandfather had purposely selected that spot. As they sat side by side, Grandfather pointed to a place on the fallen tree not far from them. From the once mighty tree now resting and decaying on the ground, Oel could see new growth. There was a new branch growing up from the log. Actually, there were several. They were not saplings growing on their own in the soil. They were growing up out of the log.

"That," said Grandfather, "is a way the forest renews itself. Nothing is ever really lost from the forest.

Whatever dies here is used to bring forth newness of life. Trees will grow, and live long lives, but eventually they will die. There are different reasons why they die. Sometimes, they die because of damage from the storms that come through, like the one we are sitting on. Sometimes, they die because of fires that sweep through the mountains. Sometimes they simply die because they are old. The same is true for shrubs and other things in the forest. It always seems sad when a grand old tree succumbs and gives up its life. But that is also something to appreciate because what made that tree becomes the nourishment for new trees to begin their lives. In the long run, you see, trees really don't give up their lives. They yield the life within their bark and branches and give it to new ones. So, life continues. On and on and on."

Oel touched one of the young trees. Its bark felt smooth and warm in the afternoon sun. Its tiny leaves were soft and supple.

Grandfather continued. "This is just like our lives, Oel. The lives of everyone in our village and elsewhere. Each of us will be born and have a beginning of life. We will grow and become tall and strong, and contribute to the beauty of our community of life. At some point in life, each of us will begin to decline. It may be very slowly or not noticeable at first, or it may strike upon us like a storm. Eventually, in some way, each of us will die. Most of us will give ourselves to new life before we pass on, though. Men and women marry and bring new life into the world in their children. Those children will grow up and become men and women who will do the same thing. The chain of life is ongoing. Those who have died left to the rest of us not just memories, but memorials to help new life live better. Those memorials may be the lands they cleared and homesteaded, or houses our ancestors built that we live in now. They may be the wells that they dug that give us the water we need to sustain living. They may be the rules they learned through hardships that we need to follow in order to live safely and fruitfully. Life doesn't give up, Oel. Some people may give up on life, but life itself will not give up."

Oel's eyes filled with tears. "I don't want you to die, Grandfather! I don't want Father or Mother or anyone to die!"

"I know, I know." said Grandfather as he gently hugged Oel. "But that is the way of life. Life on the earth, anyway. But as I said, life never gives up. It never really ends. Our faith also teaches that to us. We know from what Our Lord taught us that we have life with Him after our life on earth ends. And life with Him never ends. He had life on earth, and then died as we know and see life here. But He came back to show us life goes on and our continued life will grow up out of Him. From His death came life. That is why it is important to pray, to attend church, and read the scriptures so we can come to understand that better. I think if we do those things, then when someone dies, we will have some sadness, but we will also have some joy in knowing their life continues . . . just in a way that is different from what we know here on the earth. And, it will be such a joyful thing to live life with Our Lord, Oel."

The two sat quietly for some time on the fallen tree. Oel gently stroked the young tree emerging from the once mighty one. A quick rush of wind pushed on his face, almost like a light slap to bring him awake and almost blew off his hat. The sun was hot, and he longed for the shade of the trees still standing in the forest. A swarm of small insects buzzed by, darting back and forth, and some got just a little too close to Oel and Grandfather. The two waved their arms and hands to brush the critters away from their faces.

"Well, let's get going." said Grandfather. "The day is not waiting for us!"

It was not long before Oel and Grandfather reached the edges of the road that led back to their village. They stood quietly for a moment, looking down the road toward home and then back the other way.

Oel asked, "What is down the road that way, Grandfather?"

Grandfather replied, "About a day's walk is another village."

Oel frowned. "Will those people come to harm the people in our village?"

Grandfather gave a gentle smile. "No. They are good people. They are good like the people in our village. I have gone there sometimes to trade goods. Their ways may be a little different from ours at times, but they have goodness in their hearts. And there are other villages along the road far past theirs."

Oel wrapped his arms around Grandfather's waist. "I'm glad there are good people there!"

Grandfather then pointed across the road to where the trees parted and provided a view of the lower parts of the mountain and the valley far below. He told Oel to look at the river down in the flat regions of the valley and describe what he saw.

Oel said, "The river looks like it is winding a lot and there is nothing straight about it. It looks like it is making loops. And further downstream it looks like it splits into a bunch of smaller streams that wind back and forth, and some criss-cross with others. It's kind of like the braids in my sister's hair."

"Yes," said Grandfather. "As the river gets down to

the lowlands, the speed of its water slows a lot. It begins to meander and break into channels that twist and turn and cross into one another. They wrap around each other and intertwine. The land around and between the meanders becomes marshy. If you could see further, you would see what is called a delta. And just beyond the delta is where the river waters join the waters of the sea. It is all connected."

Oel said, "And is that part of the river like the lives of people, too?"

Grandfather smiled and replied, "Yes, it is. As people enter their older age, the flow of their lives often meanders. That doesn't mean they are confused and don't know where they are going. It actually means an opening of awareness that might not have existed before. Even though it seemed many things they did in life were distinct and separate acts at the times they were done, it now becomes clearer they were interconnected and had influences on each other that may or may not have been seen earlier in their lives. That is the time when people begin to recognize those interconnections and the real impacts of those things on the life of themselves and others. Then comes the realization that it all of it comes back together and there is really only the one direction life's river flows. It really doesn't matter how many things someone did or the paths they tried to follow when doing them. It all comes back together and ends with the river of life coming to join the great vastness of the sea that is like all of us together. What does matter is how someone helps others on their way to that sea."

The afternoon was waning and evening was not too far distant. The sun was low in the western sky yet still shone brightly. Although the heart of the day was now behind them, the road was still warm from the sun's lingering heat radiating out of the dirt, stones, and pebbles. Oel felt its warmth from the pebbles on the road as it rose up along with the dust that was stirred with each step he and Grandfather took. The forest had quieted as the animals rested and awaited the cooler part of the day. It was a time of transition, a time of change, and the breeze was stilling as it seemed to be preparing to turn and blow from a different direction. There was a definite change in the feel of it all. Something, Oel felt, was coming to an end . . . and something else was getting ready to begin. Oel realized this was really what life was. What was in the mountains and forest was just like what was in his own life and that of everyone he knew. He and Grandfather turned toward home. The last part of their walk would be completed in a short time, and they would be home for dinner.

## CHAPTER 9

## THE END OF DRAGONS

Oel could tell Grandfather was tired. His pace had slowed and there was not as much spring in his step as earlier. There was just the slightest slump in his shoulders and faint traces of sagging in his face. Oel felt tired, too. He hoped Grandfather did not see it. He imagined the two of them entering the door of the house like energetic victors returning from an odyssey. But Grandfather was keenly observant and could see the fatigue dragging on Oel. So, they kept the pace of their walking slow and tried to walk on the side of the road covered in the shadows cast by the trees. The road home seemed longer than it was when they departed a couple of days before. The pebbles seemed slightly larger, enough so to cause an unwary foot to stumble a little bit. The tips of their walking staffs were dragging some in the dirt behind them. Oel listened to the scuffing of his feet, to the heaviness of his breathing, and the rhythm of his heartbeat. He started counting to see if his steps matched the beats of his heart. Then, he stopped and gently stirred the dust on the road with his toes.

"Grandfather," Oel asked, "Earlier today, I asked you if there was still dragon sign anywhere. Are the dragons still here?"

Grandfather paused. "I asked those same questions when I was your age. I think at some point everyone asks them."

"Are there answers to them?" queried Oel.

"I believe there are." responded Grandfather. "I believe there is still dragon sign, all around us, if we choose to try seeing it."

"What are they, Grandfather?" Oel pried.

The two stepped to the side of the road and sat down with their backs against a large tree that shaded them from the sun.

Grandfather inhaled deeply. "Let's first speak about the red dragon. Red dragon sign spreads everywhere when the sun shines orange and red in the mornings and evenings. Every time you see lightning from the sky, you are seeing red dragon sign. The forest fires that sometimes rage through the mountains and valleys are red dragon sign. Each time you see the hot red iron being hammered in the blacksmith's shop, that is red dragon sign. When you see into the depths of the flames in the fireplace at home, you are seeing red dragon sign. I also think when you feel fire in your heart for something, like burning love, that is red dragon sign."

Oel said, "I do see those things, Grandfather. But I never thought of them as being from the red dragon!"

Grandfather smiled and continued. "Now, lets' speak

about the blue dragon. The blue dragon sign is in every lake, pond, and stream. We saw it throughout the day, from the waterfall to the meanders down in the flats of the valley below. The flow of the waters can change the land, just as the blue dragon sometimes did. When we see clouds with torrential rains, we are seeing blue dragon sign. The raging storms at sea and on the great lakes are blue dragon sign, and sometimes they are helpful and sometimes cause the wrecking of ships. I think there is blue dragon sign in the mists, and in the dew that forms on the grass in the mornings. I remember today when you shed tears about me and others. Those watery tears are blue dragon sign."

"So," Oel said, "we live amongst and carry with us blue dragon sign?"

"Yes," said Grandfather. "Now, about brown dragon sign. We have been walking on brown dragon sign all these past few days. The mountains are brown dragon sign, as are the caves and rocks and stones that seem to be everywhere. The roads and paths upon which we walk, the dirt and the dust and the pebbles, all are brown dragon sign. Whenever we find landslides, we are finding brown dragon sign. And earthquakes . . . the earthquakes . . . those are brown dragon sign, too. The soils back home in which we plant our crops are brown dragon sign."

Oel turned his head to look at the mountain around them, and then at the road at his feet. "I didn't know so much was from the brown dragon!"

Grandfather said, "Remember that it is not so much from the dragon as it is what was given to the dragon to use by God." Dragon sign is a reflection of what God has created and sent into the world. The dragons were just one way for God to touch the earth."

"So, what about white dragon sign, Grandfather? What about white dragon sign?" asked Oel anxiously.

"Now that is very special!" said Grandfather. "The brilliance of the sun's beams and reflections off anything, like the palisades, are white dragon sign. The white clouds in the sky, the fluffy ones and the wispy ones, are white dragon sign. The colors of the ice in glaciers to the north and in the snow that falls in winter are white dragon sign. The glittering of light you see in diamonds, or sapphires, or any gemstone are white dragon sign. The glimmer of hope and love in someone's eyes are white dragon sign."

Oel slowly nodded his head up and down.

"All of those dragon sign, all of it, is from the breath of the dragons. And there is something more about the dragons, Oel, that you must remember."

"What is that, Grandfather?"

"Each of them was created by God with a good heart.

God created each of them for a special purpose. And each of them had their hearts corrupted by the touch of Lucifer." said Grandfather. "Each of the dragons made choices about what to do with the powers with which they were endowed. The red dragon, the blue dragon, and the brown dragon each let the goodness of their hearts yield at times to the darkness. Because of that, their hearts became heavier and blacker, and they chose to use their powers to cause harm to others through vindictiveness or vengeance."

"But each of the four dragons caused harm to others Even the white dragon!" said Oel with a puzzled look.

"True!" said Grandfather. "But you must look at how each dragon used its powers and its intent in using that power. The red, blue, and brown dragons each let their anger overtake them, and they used their powers to punish and have revenge on people. That was not the case for the white dragon. The white dragon used its power to stop darkness, but did not do it out of anger or meanness. That kept the Lucifer spot on its heart from growing and taking over its heart."

"People must make those same kinds of choices, right Grandfather?" asked Oel as he raised one eyebrow.

"Yes, people must. Each of us must choose right from wrong, and each of us must choose how to act in doing what is right as well as doing what is wrong. Every day, we are each faced with walking in the light or walking in the dark. The dark is insidious, and often begins very small and unassuming in things, and it is easy to believe we are conducting acts of the light when we are not. Each time we act with ill intent, no matter how small and trivial it may be, that darkness will grow. And as it grows, it makes us more likely to draw upon it the next time and the next, and let it guide us in our thoughts and actions. All of it, Oel, is dragon sign. The question each of us must answer is how we make use of that dragon sign."

Oel was quiet for a while, and then asked, "So, are the dragons still here? Still on the earth and still with us? Where are they?"

Grandfather paused a minute. "The dragons are no longer here as they were described in the legends. They are gone. The only thing that remains of them is their breath that we see in dragon sign."

"So, what happened to them?" asked Oel.

"Nobody really knows for sure, Oel." Grandfather said. "Some people say they went to rest and never awakened again. Some say the dragons dissolved and faded away, and the elements from which they were created spread back into the realms from which they were taken at the beginning. But they disappeared at the same time. The disappeared because they were not needed any longer. It was the end of dragons."

"Oel queried, "Why were they not needed any longer?"

Grandpa smiled a tired smile. "They were no longer needed because The Child came."

"The Child?" asked a puzzled Oel.

"Yes," said Grandfather. "The Child. The Child of God the Father. Jesus. Everything that was good in the dragons was in The Child. And there was even more goodness in The Child than any dragons could possibly contain. When The Child came to us, it was His goodness and His power that worked in the world. It was His graces that brought God's true light here. It was through His sacrifice for us that He gave us life."

Oel breathed in deeply. "All these years I have heard that. I guess I never really understood what it all really meant. But I see it now, Grandfather. I understand." He paused. "Thank you, Grandfather, for helping me understand."

Grandfather embraced Oel, and the two held tightly and hugged each other. Grandfather kissed Oel on the top of his head, and then took hold of his hand. Then, they stood up and walked the rest of the way home.

Father, Mother and Sister had just completed their prayer for the evening meal when there was a knock on the door. Each looked up and at the others, and Father quickly scooted back his bench and stood upright. He turned to the door and took a step toward it. Then there was another knock. The thick wood of the oak door made the knock sound more like a thump. Father's hand reached out and gripped the doorknob and turned it. The huge door slowly opened, its hinges groaning and the wood creaking. There, in the light of the setting sun, stood two figures. He knew immediately who they were. Oel laughed and said, "It's about time you opened this door!" Grandfather and Father laughed, too. The two stepped into the house across the threshold and tossed their satchels, hats, and blanket rolls to the side of the door. They propped their walking sticks against the wall. Mother and Sister rushed to greet them with hugs.

"Come, join us for supper!" said Mother.

"That sounds wonderful!" said Grandfather.

"It sure does!" exclaimed Oel.

Everyone sat down around the table and another prayer was said. It was a prayer for the food, but also in thanksgiving for Grandfather and Oel being brought back home safely. Oel looked at the fire quietly burning in the fireplace, then at the stones that made the walls of their house, and then at the old wooden buckets filled with water sitting by the table. Then, he looked and saw the glittering in Mother's eyes, and the beaming smiles from Father and Sister. The dragon sign was in it all.

And in her gentle softness, Mother spoke with a smile and a tear in her eye. "Two days ago, our child departed from this house. He is gone and will never come back. But that is okay, because now we have a new man with us! And that is such a wonderfully loving sign the Lord has given to breathe newness into our lives!"

www.ingramcontent.com/pod-product-compliance
Ingram Content Group UK Ltd.
Pitfield, Milton Keynes, MK11 3LW, UK
UKHW041946230426
12048UKWH00008B/158